DISNEY · PIXAR

UXBRIDGE COLLEGE

Learning Resource Centre
Park Road, Uxbridge, Middlesex, UB8 1NQ
Renewals: 01895 853344

Please return this item to the LRC on or before the last date stamped **below:**

2 0 FEB 2018

2 8 JUN 2021

D1320370

This edition published 2017 by Paper Rocket
an imprint of Parragon Books Ltd.
Paper Rocket logo and name ™ Parragon Books Ltd

Parragon Books Ltd
Chartist House
15–17 Trim Street
Bath BA1 1HA, UK
www.parragon.com

ISBN 978-1-4748-7191-4

Printed in the UK

BOOK of the FILM

By Suzanne Francis

PAPER ROCKET

Stories that take you to another world

CHAPTER 1

Lightning McQueen closed his eyes and concentrated on the sound of his breathing. "Okay, here we go," he said to himself. "Focus." He took a deep breath. "Speed. I am speed," he said, and he imagined racing around a track to the sound of a packed stadium. "One winner. Forty-two losers. I eat losers for breakfast."

He pictured more cars whipping around the track. "Did I used to say that? Really?" he said, suddenly realizing how silly it sounded.

"Yeah. Ya did," said Mater.

Lightning screamed, surprised by Mater's interruption of his pre-race ritual. "Mater?" he asked.

"Hey, Buddy!" Mater replied. "Yep, you used to say that all the time. I remember this one time –"

Lightning cut him off. "Mater! What are you doing in here?"

"Just wanted to wish ya good luck," he said.

"Well, thank you," Lightning said, softening a bit. "But I need a little quiet. I'm kinda preparing for a race."

Just then, the door on Mack's trailer began to lower.

"Oh, right!" Mater said. "Sorry. Good luck with psychin' yourself up!" He started to leave, but turned back when he saw the open trailer door. "Open or closed?" he asked.

"Closed, please," Lightning said.

"You got it, buddy!" Mater shouted as he left.

The door closed and Lightning took a deep breath. "Okay," he said, settling back into his routine. "I am speed –"

But Mater's voice interrupted him again. Only this time, Lightning could hear him yelling outside the trailer. "Hey!" Mater called. "My best friend, Lightning McQueen, needs quiet! Perfect quiet! Got it?"

Lightning chuckled, then gave himself a moment to get back into the zone. "Okay, where was I?" he asked. After another deep breath, he said, "Racing. Real racing."

In his mind, he saw himself racing again – but this time he was back at home in Radiator Springs, whizzing around the quiet, expansive Willy's Butte with his old friend and mentor, Doc Hudson.

Even though Doc had been gone for some time, Lightning could still hear his gruff voice, clear as day. As he remembered the scene, he could hear Doc say, "That ain't racing. That wasn't even a Sunday drive. That was one lap. Racing is five hundred of those. Everybody's fighting to move up, lap after lap – inside, outside, inches apart, never touching. Now that's racin'!"

"Wow," Lightning whispered. He was back in the present moment, and looking at a picture of him and Doc.

The trailer doors opened and Lightning slipped out. "All right, here we go! This one's for you, Doc!" He revved his engine and took off.

Bright sunlight sparkled down on the Florida International Super Speedway as Lightning blazed past the larger-than-life screen. He had hit the track at full speed. The race had started, the place was packed, and Lightning's fans exploded with cheers when they saw the flash of red streak by. But there was one enthusiastic young fan that stood out from the crowd. Her name was Maddy and she seemed to shout Lightning's name louder than anyone.

Lightning's best friends from Radiator Springs were in the stands too. They cheered loudly – but no one was more excited than Mater. He tried to get as close as possible, weaving through the crowd, saying, "'Scuze me, pardon me. Best friend coming through!" All while wearing a hat with a large, yellow foam lightning bolt ... that looked like it was going through his head. "Go, McQueen!" he shouted.

Up ahead, Lightning could see his longtime top rivals: Bobby Swift and Cal Weathers. As he narrowed the gap, he saw another racer, Brick Yardley. Lightning cruised up next to his friend and saw an opportunity to get him off his game: "Hey, Cal. Gas cap's open."

"Oh, what?" Cal replied. He realized Lightning was joking, then quickly added, "Hey! Well, your gas cap's open!"

"Good comeback," Bobby retorted.

Lightning couldn't help but laugh as he led his friends around the back stretch of the track. The style of racing was beautiful, and the fans cheered, loving every second.

As they headed towards the pits, announcers Bob Cutlass and Darrell Cartrip commented on the friendly rivalry. "And into the pit goes Lightning McQueen, Bobby Swift and Cal Weathers," Bob said. "These three are fun to watch, aren't they, Darrell?"

"I can't tell if they have more fun on or off the track!" Darrell replied.

Lightning pulled into his station and Guido got to work. Rusty and Dusty of Rust-eze, Lightning's longtime sponsor, proudly watched as Guido swiftly changed Lightning's tyres.

"All right, Guido," said Dusty. "You move faster than my brother leaks oil," he laughed at his own clever joke.

Sally and Mater watched close by, and Lightning winked at Sally as Guido finished up.

"*Finito!*" Guido yelled, tightening the last bolt on a new set of racing tyres. "*Via! Via!*" And with that, Lightning took off – burning ahead of Cal, Bobby and Brick.

"You gettin' a car wash, too, Cal?" Lightning called back.

"No! You're gettin' a car wash, McQueen!" yelled Cal.

Lightning blistered around the last turn and towards the finish line. Both Bobby and Cal were a length behind, on either side of him. The chequered flag dropped and the crowd burst into cheers. Lightning McQueen had won again.

Lightning loved racing, and he felt especially great after winning! He entered the pits and moved towards the garage while Shannon Spokes interviewed him about the win.

"Lightning, this was your second win in three races," Shannon said. "How do you keep your focus?"

"Well, it's really just that I –"

But before he could answer, his eyes caught a glimpse of something menacing just outside the frame of Shannon Spokes' interview camera.

"Bobby! Cal! No no no! Noooooooooo!" Lightning yelled.

Whoosh! All of a sudden, Lightning was hit with the foam blast of a fire extinguisher, then immediately peppered with antenna balls. Lightning found himself looking ridiculous and completely unprofessional on camera, while Bobby and Cal wheeled away and laughed hysterically.

"Oh, they're gonna pay," Lightning whispered.

Days later, at the Heartland Motor Speedway, Cal, Lightning, Bobby and Brick were at it again. The rivals were locked in a tight finish, but this time Cal had won! As they swarmed the pits, Cal's Dinoco pit crew cheered.

After the race, Cal cruised through the crowd to get to Victory Lane. Just like after Lightning's win, he was being interviewed by Shannon Spokes, and the conversation was projected on the large screen.

"Great win today, Cal," Shannon said.

"Thank you, Shannon –"

Screech!

" – it was a great day out there –"

Screech!

" – and I'd like to thank my sp–"

Screech!

As Cal tried to answer Shannon, he kept getting interrupted by loud, mechanical sounds. And he didn't realize it at the time, but as he spoke, he slowly started to rise higher and higher ... so much so that it became impossible for Shannon to continue her interview. Cal then looked down and discovered that his tyres had been replaced with enormous inflatable ones – thanks to Guido and his quick-change abilities!

"Hey. Hey! Guido!" Cal yelled.

Guido blew smoke off his prized tyre spanner. "Pit stop," he said.

"Real funny, guys," Cal replied.

Lightning and Bobby raced away, laughing loudly. Cal tried to chase after them – but his wheels wouldn't rotate. Left with no other choice, he unsuccessfully hopped and bounced in their general direction. "Guys! I'm not gonna fit in the trailer like this," he called out.

After a short break in the season, Lightning found himself back in Radiator Springs. The sun shone brightly on the landscape as Lightning took a quick training run around Willy's Butte. He effortlessly sailed past Mater, Sheriff, Guido and Luigi. Sheriff checked Lightning's speed while the others cheered him on. Guido and Mater even had matching baseball caps with lightning bolts and the number 95 plastered on top.

"Keep it going, buddy!" Mater yelled.

And just like that, Lightning was back on the road, racing his best and pulling out another win. As Lightning drove through pit row, he called out to Rusty and Dusty: "Are my sponsors happy today?"

"No, man!" Dusty replied. "Stop winning, will ya? We're running out of bumper cream to sell!"

Just then, The King – Dinoco's former number one racer (and Cal's predecessor) – and Tex, Dinoco's longtime owner – rolled up alongside Lightning. "Hey, good race today, Lightning!" The King said.

"Mr The King! Hey, Big Tex! How's my favourite competitor?" Lightning asked.

"Offer still stands," said Tex. "Just say the word, and you can be my number one car at Team Dinoco."

They rolled past Tex's trailer and Cal popped out from inside.

"You know I can hear you, right?" shouted Cal. "I'm right here!"

Lightning chuckled. Tex joked this way with Lightning every time they saw each other. "Bye, Cal!" he said. "See you next week … or not!"

Days later, at the Motor Speedway of the South, Lightning led a tight pack of cars around the track.

"Another great finish in the making!" shouted announcer Bob Cutlass. "Lightning and Swift, nose to nose."

"How's the view from back there, Bobby?" Lightning joked as he zoomed ahead.

"Ha, ha!" chuckled Bobby. "Well, you better not blink. I'll blow right past ya!"

The fans bubbled with excitement, afraid to miss a beat of the thrillingly close race. "The flag is out!" yelled Bob Cutlass. "It's the final stretch! Lightning is in the lead...."

Fueled by the sounds of the crowd, Lightning smiled as he focused on the track ahead, determined to hold his position. "Okay, let's see what you got!" he called back to Bobby, prodding him to pick up his pace. He and his racing friends loved the challenge of beating someone at their best. And part of the fun of racing was pushing each other to go faster.

"*Whoo-weee!*" yelled Bobby, feeding off Lightning and trying to get closer to him.

Just then, a strange new car appeared right behind Bobby. He was a young, modern-looking racer. On his black body were electric blue details and the number 2.0. Before Bobby and Lightning knew what had happened, the sleek car made a sudden move and effortlessly surged past both of them, grabbing the win! Lightning couldn't believe it. The car had come out of nowhere.

CHAPTER 2

"Oh, my!" said Bob Cutlass, shocked. "It's Jackson Storm for the win! A huge upset!"

The other announcer, Darrell Cartrip, chimed in: "Neither Lightnin' nor Bobby ever saw him comin'!"

Lightning rolled to a stop in front of his Rust-eze pit crew. He watched the replay on the large screen as the track announcer excitedly reported over the PA, "Wow, what a finish. Even the crowd seems stunned. I don't remember the last time a racer came out of the blue to win it. It's one thing to start fast, but we haven't seen anyone cross the line with that kind of speed and power since a young Lightning McQueen first arrived on the scene."

While the other racing cars headed back to their trailers, Lightning lingered for a moment, still completely taken aback. He never would have predicted that was how the race would end. Where did that car come from?

He left the track and slowly made his way towards his hauler. Before he reached it, he turned to see Storm emerge from his modern-looking trailer. Storm barely glanced at Lightning as he revved his powerful engine and continued driving. Bobby and Brick approached Lightning, and they watched the reporters swarm Storm.

"Hey, Bobby? Who is that?" asked Lightning.

"That's, um … Jackson Storm," answered Bobby.

"Yeah, one of the rookies," added Cal.

Reporters bombarded Storm with compliments and questions. "That was incredible! Awesome! Give me a few words!" they shouted. "Can we get a picture here?"

"Thank you, guys," said Storm, expressionless. "Thank you. No. I appreciate it. Thank you very much. Thank you."

Storm rolled past Lightning and came to a stop where his crew chief and pitties were waiting for him. Lightning approached with a friendly smile. "Hey – Jackson Storm, right?" he said. "Great race today."

Storm turned to Lightning and looked at him with a cold, competitive glare. Then he spoke in a voice that sounded like a starstruck fan. "Wow! Thank you, Lightning McQueen. You have no idea what a pleasure it is for me to finally beat you."

"Oh, thanks!" said Lightning. Storm turned away, and Lightning's face fell as he realized what Storm had just said. "Wait. Hang on.... Did you say 'meet' or 'beat'?"

Storm inched closer to Lightning. "I think you heard me."

"Uh, what?" said Lightning, shocked by Storm's attitude.

Some photographers rushed over, ready to snap some photos. "Lightning! Storm! Over here!

"Yeah, yeah, come on," said Storm, smiling big. "Let's get a picture! You know what? Get a ton of pictures! Because Champ here has been a role model of mine for years now! And I mean a lot of years! Right? I love this guy!"

The reporters and photographers continued to shout and compete for Storm's attention. After posing for a few shots Storm rolled towards his trailer. "I think I touched a nerve," he mumbled as he passed his crew chief. He backed into his trailer, and loud music began to blare as the gate closed. The truck pulled away and Lightning was alone, stunned and speechless.

CHAPTER 3

"Welcome back to Chick's Picks with Chick Hicks!" shouted Racing Sports Network television host Chick Hicks. He wore a big grin as he stood beside his Piston Cup in front of a wall-sized screen. "I'm your host, former-and-forever Piston Cup Champion, Chick Hicks. Doot-doot-doot-do! This just in: Rookie Jackson Storm slams the proverbial door on Lightning McQueen. Ooooh, I couldn't have enjoyed it more if I'd beaten Lightning myself. Oh, wait, I have!"

On the screen flashed a photo of Lightning's shocked expression when he lost to Storm.

"But enough about me," continued Chick. "Here to tell you how it happened is professional number-cruncher Miss Natalie Certain!"

The camera widened to reveal a smart, confident, ruby-coloured car standing at the other end of the screen. "It's a pleasure to be here, Chick," said Natalie. "And actually, I prefer the term 'statistical analyst'."

"Right. So ... who is this mysterious newcomer, Jackson Storm, and why is he so darn fast?" asked Chick.

Statistics and other information suddenly filled the screen behind them as Natalie explained: "It's no mystery if you study the data, Mr Hicks. Jackson Storm is part of the next generation of high-tech racers – unlike the veterans of yesterday."

Chick pulled up the photo of Lightning's face again, and it flashed close up so that the viewers at home could see him. "What? Old-timers like this guy?" He chuckled.

"Um … right," said Natalie, getting back to business. "Storm achieves his top speeds by exploiting the numbers." A picture of Storm appeared. "I refer, of course, to racing data," she said, rolling her eyes at the sight of the picture. "Tyre pressure, down force, weight distribution, aerodynamics … and Next Gens – like Storm – are taking advantage. The racing world is changing."

Chick smiled. "And for the better, if it means my old rival, Lightning, is down for the count. Am I right, Certain?"

"Well, if I'm certain of anything, Chick, it's that this season is about to get even more interesting," said Natalie.

The following night, an anxious crowd at the speedway roared with anticipation as racers ran the pace lap under the moon's glow.

Above the track, inside the little booth in the tower, Bob Cutlass and Darrell Cartrip watched, analyzing the action below. "I'll tell you what, Darrell," said Bob Cutlass, looking down on the track. "Jackson Storm has certainly made an impact…. We've got six more next-generation rookies in the field …"

"… with six veterans fired to clear the way," added Darrell.

The six new racers were in sync as they headed towards the green flag. In a way, it was like they were all variations of the same car.

Storm was up in front, in the pole position, and Lightning was right beside him. "Morning, Champ," said Storm. "And how's our living legend today?"

"Uh, still very much alive, thank you, and I would appreciate –" Lightning started.

"You know," said Storm, interrupting him, "I can't believe I get to race *the* Lightning McQueen in his farewell season."

"What are you talking about?" Lightning asked.

"Oops, green flag. Good luck out there, champ! You're gonna need it."

The flag dropped, and Storm took off. Lightning angrily revved his engine and raced after him.

More next-gen rookies appeared around Lightning, effortlessly moving ahead of him. They seemed to race with robotic precision. As hard as he tried, Lightning couldn't pull in front. He continued to push himself and managed to get ahead of some of the rookies, but Storm held the lead. As the flag dropped and the race ended, Storm was the first to finish again.

Even though Lightning had given his all, he came in third.

Meanwhile, at the Racing Sports Network studio, Natalie Certain and Chick Hicks continued to discuss her research on his show: "One reason Storm and the Next Gens are more efficient? Their ability to hold the optimum racing line every single lap."

Over the next few days, the racing world buzzed as Storm continued to win race after race. And as Storm's winning streak wore on, Lightning became more and more frustrated. Reporters couldn't stop talking about Storm. Natalie Certain's show, Morning Piston Cup, had more viewers than ever. In fact, every show on the Racing Sports Network had something to say about the amazing new rookie.

Lightning couldn't get through a minute of his day without hearing something about Storm.

Natalie Certain was constantly analyzing his every move: "Storm's in a class of his own, and a big reason for that? Training on the newest cutting-edge simulators." As she spoke, the camera showed footage of Storm on a high-tech simulator. "These machines create a virtual racing experience that is so real, these racers never even have to go outside," she explained.

Meanwhile, on Chick Hicks's show, he was interviewing Storm in the field. "Piston Cup winner Chick Hicks here – with the racer who is taking the circuit by storm! Jackson Storm!" Chick flashed a big smile as he stood beside Storm in Victory Lane at Flathead Motor Speedway. "Another easy win over old Ka-chow – or should I say Ka-boose? 'Cause he's always in the back! Am I right?"

Out in the trailer area, Lightning looked up at the large screen as he rolled by. He stopped to listen to Storm's answer.

"No, no, no, Chick," answered Storm. "Lightning is a crafty veteran champ. He's the elder statesman of the sport, ya know? Takes everything I got to beat him."

"Oh, you gotta be kidding me," Lightning said to himself, irritated. When he turned away from the large screen, he saw his sponsors, Rusty and Dusty. They were surrounded by a pack of reporters.

"Rusty and Dusty!" shouted the reporters. They began to shoot a series of questions at them.

"What changes are you going to make to get Lightning McQueen back on top?" said one.

"Will Lightning try new training methods?" asked another.

"Is he prepared to retire? Are you prepared to retire him?" asked yet another.

Lightning rolled over to try to help as Rusty and Dusty stammered. "Come on guys," said Lightning. "Let's not overreact. It's just a slump. We'll get 'em next week."

The reporters immediately swarmed towards Lightning. "Over here!" shouted one. "Hey, Lightning!" shouted another.

"Okay, that's enough," Lightning said, trying to make them stop. "No comment."

"Not even about Cal Weathers retiring?" asked one reporter.

"Wait, what?" asked Lightning, stopping in his tracks.

"Cal Weathers. He's hanging up his Lightyears," said the reporter.

"No," said Lightning. "No comment on that, either."

Lightning rushed over to Cal, who was backing into his trailer. "Hey, Cal? Hey! Retirement? What's going on?"

Cal smiled when he saw Lightning. "I asked my uncle once how I'd know when it was time to stop," he answered. "Ya know what he said? The youngsters'll tell ya."

Lightning didn't know how to respond.

Just as the door to Cal's trailer began to close, he added, "We had some good times together. Gonna miss that the most, I think."

"Yeah," said Lightning.

Cal disappeared behind the door and Lightning was left alone. A wave of shock and sadness washed over him. How could Cal be done? How was it that Lightning would never get another chance to race with him? Lightning stood there frozen, watching as the truck drove off. He would give anything to go back to the way it was ... before Storm was on the scene.

CHAPTER 4

Later that night, the racing news programmes continued to cover the next-gen racers and discuss the drastic changes that were happening to the sport of racing. On the set of The Morning Piston Cup, Natalie Certain stood beside the giant screen. It was filled with a grid showing the 40 Piston Cup racers at the start of the season. The veteran racers were on illuminated squares.

"More changes ahead, Chick," said Natalie. "Every week, we've seen veteran racers either retire, like Cal Weathers tonight, or be fired to make room for these younger, faster racers. And it's not over yet." As she continued to explain, more and more squares went dark, signifying the departure of those cars from the racing circuit.

But Lightning refused to give up. And the final race, at the Los Angeles International Speedway, seemed like the perfect place to get out of his slump and back on top. That morning, a team of jets streaked across the blue sky as excitement grew in the crowded stands. An announcer's voice boomed over the PA.

"Hello, racing fans," he said. "Welcome to the Los Angeles 500! Final race of the Piston Cup season! It's been a year of surprises, and today promises to be no different. While the teams get ready in the pits, we get ready to bring you the action here, trackside."

Lightning was on his way to Bobby's garage, then stopped when he noticed Brick and his sponsor heading down the middle of the garage area. Two pitties carried big boxes with Brick's name scribbled across their sides. Lightning began to move towards Brick, but stopped short when he saw him talking urgently to his sponsor.

"You can't do this!" yelled Brick. "I've raced for you guys for almost ten years!"

"Sorry, Brick," said the sponsor. "My mind's made up. Time for me to move on to someone new."

"Hey! I … I had two wins last year!" Brick cried.

"The whole sport's changing," said the sponsor. "I'm just doing what I gotta do."

Lightning turned to see a racer pulling out of Bobby's garage and went to him. "Hey, Bobby?" he said. "Do you know what's happening with Brick?" But Lightning quickly realized – it wasn't Bobby in Bobby's garage. It was another racer. A new, next-gen racer.

"The name's Danny, bro," said the sleek racing car as he headed past Lightning. Lightning looked around the garage area and couldn't believe his eyes: there was no one but next-gen racers all around. He didn't recognize any of them. *What was going on? How could everything be changing so fast?* he thought.

Lightning left the garage and took the pace lap, finding himself in the third row, next to Daniel.

"Hey, champ," said Storm, calling to Lightning from the front. "Where'd all your friends go?"

"A final check of his tyres as Storm settles into the pole position," Bob Cutlass said over the PA.

Lightning tried to contain his anger while Storm scrubbed his tyres and moved to take his position on the pole.

The green flag flew – it was time to race – and Darrell Cartrip's voice came over the speakers. "Boogity, boogity, boogity! Let's end this season with a great race!"

Sally and the Radiator Springs gang watched nervously.

"That's it, Buddy!" cheered Mater as Lightning leaned hard into a sprint.

The race went on into the night. Storm held the lead, with Lightning a few lengths behind. As Storm led the racers into the pits, Shannon Spokes reported from the sidelines: "Forty laps to go, and race leader, Jackson Storm, is making his way onto pit road, with McQueen on his tail," she said. "A good stop here could mean the difference between victory and defeat."

Storm's swift, efficient pit crew immediately got to work.

At the same time, Guido worked as quickly as he could on Lightning. The racer was antsy.

"C'mon, c'mon, c'mon!" he said, panic in his voice. "Faster, Guido! C'mon, I gotta get back out there before he does! Guido, hurry up!"

Within seconds, Guido had finished! "Fatto! Fatto!" he said, moving away. Lightning got back out before any of the other racers.

"What a pit stop by Lightning McQueen!" shouted Darrell Cartrip. "Man! He just got the lead!"

"But, Darrell – can he hold on to it?" asked Bob Cutlass.

Before long, Storm pulled alongside Lightning. "Hey, Lightning," he said. "You all right? Listen, don't you worry, pal. You had a good run. Enjoy your retirement." Then he effortlessly sped ahead.

"Storm takes back the lead!" said Bob Cutlass. "A length in front."

Furious, Lightning pushed himself forward, harder and harder, using everything he had to try to catch Storm.

"Unbelievable!" yelled Darrell Cartrip. "Lightning is fading! Lightning is fading! Fading fast!"

"No! No, no, no, no!" shouted Lightning, straining as he tried to get ahead. Now he was two lengths behind Storm. Lightning angrily pushed himself harder until … one of his tyres blew out! He started to spin! Whipping around and around, everything went blurry, and a deafening hush came over the crowd.

In the stands, Sally gasped. She and the rest of the Radiator Springs gang held their breath as they helplessly watched Lightning's spin turn into a roll. The fans were completely silent as the entire stadium witnessed the worst crash of Lightning's career. With every flip, they could hear the terrible crunch of Lightning's body against the pavement. He continued to roll and roll until, finally, he stopped, a low hiss of smoke rising from his engine. Suddenly, a flurry of activity appeared, surrounding him. An ambulance, a fire engine and a tow truck rushed to his aid while the crowd watched, horrified – hoping to see signs of life.

CHAPTER 5

Four months had passed since Lightning's devastating crash. He had survived and was recovering at home in Radiator Springs. But in all that time, he hadn't so much as raced a lap. Some music played through a tinny radio speaker inside Doc's garage.

"Welcome back to Piston Cup Talk Round the Clock, where we do nothing but talk racing," said the radio show's host, Mike Joyride. "So let's get to it, starting, of course, with Lightning McQueen. The season start is just two weeks away, and there's still no official announcement. But with number 95 coming off his worst year on record – don't shoot the messenger here, folks – I think it's safe to assume that Lightning McQueen's racing days are over. Meanwhile, Jackson Storm is looking even faster than –"

Lightning clicked off the radio, took a deep breath, and let out a big, long sigh. It was clear he wasn't himself, and that he wasn't doing well. He eyed the dusty old film projector in the corner of the garage and rolled over to it. He flipped a switch and it came to life, flickering and flashing old racing footage against the wall.

The commentator's voice shouted above the sound of the old, roaring engines: "As they enter the final lap, the number 6 and number 12 cars are still fighting it out for the lead. But wait! Here he comes! It's the Fabulous Hudson Hornet knocking on their door! What's he got up his sleeve today?"

Lightning couldn't help smiling at the sight of Doc racing on the track.

"And there it is!" the announcer continued. "With one incredible move, he's past them! As they take the final turn, the Hornet takes a decisive lead! He's flying up the straightaway. He's left the pack behind! His crew chief, Smokey, is loving it! It's unbelievable!" But then panic crept into the announcer's voice. "Oh, no! He's in trouble! The Hudson Hornet has lost control!"

Lightning watched as Doc spun out. It was long and painful to see Doc spin, roll, and finally crash. The emergency personnel rushed onto the track as the commentator continued: "A tragic day for racing. It's hard to believe the number 51 will ever come back from a crash like this."

Lightning stopped the film. As he did so, he remembered a conversation he had with Doc years before, in the exact spot where he was currently parked.

"You think I quit?" asked Doc, frustrated. "They quit on me. When I finally got put together, I went back, expecting a big welcome. You know what they said? 'You're history.' Moved right on to the next rookie standing in line." Doc took a breath. "There was a lot left in me I never got a chance to show 'em."

"Hey, Stickers," said Sally, rolling into the garage. Her voice shook Lightning out of his memory.

"Hey, Sal," he said quietly.

"So … how ya feeling?" she asked, wearing a look of concern. It was also clear that she had an agenda.

"Yeah. Great. Really, really great," Lightning replied, his voice dripping with sarcasm.

"Thinking about Doc again?"

"Yeah," said Lightning, looking down at the floor. "You know, they told him when he was done. He didn't decide." He sighed heavily before continuing. "I don't want what happened to Doc to happen to me."

"But that hasn't happened," she replied.

"No. But I can't go out on the track and do the same old thing. It won't work."

"Then change it up," said Sally. "Try something new."

Lightning was unconvinced. "I don't know, Sally, I –"

"Don't fear failure," she interrupted. "Be afraid of not having the chance. You have the chance. Doc didn't." She paused for a moment, wanting her words to sink in. "And you can either take it, or you can do what you've been doing – sitting in here for months...." She looked around the garage as she continued, the playful tone back in her voice. "And by the way, I love what you've done with the place. I mean, the monster-movie lighting. The, uh, musky air freshener. And don't let anyone tell you you're not working that primer – because, wow – I've never found you more attractive. And now that I've been in here for a couple minutes … the stench … I'm getting kind of used to it –"

"Okay, okay, Sal," Lightning said. "I get it."

"I miss you, Lightning. We all do."

"Try something new. Huh," Lightning repeated, mulling over Sally's words.

Just then, Mater burst in. "Hey, did it work, Miss Sally?" he asked. "Did you set him straight with your lawyerly powers of persuasion?"

Sally looked at Lightning, waiting for him to answer.

"Is he ready to start trainin'?" Mater asked, looking at Lightning, too.

"Well, Stinky – eh, Stickers?" she asked, a smile in her voice.

"Yes, Mater, I am," said Lightning with a chuckle. He was grateful to have such good friends.

"*Whooooooo-hoo-hoo-hoo!*" yelped Mater.

"I decide when I'm done," he said to Sally.

"I was hoping you'd say that."

"Okay, but I got an idea, and I'm gonna need to talk to Rusty and Dusty, all right?" said Lightning.

"I'll get 'em on the horn!" said Mater, rushing off. "Get it? On the horn!" He laughed out loud as he honked his horn, driving the joke home even harder. He suddenly stopped laughing and scrunched up his nose. "Oops, hold on, I gotta sneeze," he said, moving his chassis and grille around. He sighed. "Dadgum, I lost it! Hey, I'll see ya at Flo's." He left, but was only gone a second when they heard a loud "Ah-choo!" and then "I found it!"

Lightning and Sally looked at each other and burst out laughing. Lightning felt great. He was ready to start racing again.

CHAPTER 6

A little while later at the V8 Café, Flo, Mater and the rest of the Radiator Springs gang were gathered around a monitor having a video call with Rusty and Dusty.

"What about the car from Everett?" asked Rusty, already chuckling at the thought of him. "Remember him?"

"He was stuck in reverse!" said Dusty. "I said, 'You need a house with a circular driveway!'"

Rusty and Dusty burst out laughing, and Flo laughed, too. "You boys need to get your rusty tails down here," she said. "I created a drink in your honour."

"Yeah!" said Mater. "The Rust-eze Medicated Bumper Bomb. It goes down faster than a lift full of Winnebagos!"

Rusty and Dusty laughed at Mater's joke as Lightning arrived with Sally. Everyone in the café lit up and gave Lightning a hearty welcome. They were happy to see him out and about. Lightning looked around and saw everyone. Then it suddenly got very quiet. "Wow. You're all here," he said.

"Sorry, buddy," said Mater. "Did you want this call to be private?"

"No, Mater – this is perfect." Lightning took a deep breath before continuing. "Listen – thanks, everyone, for sticking by me. It took me a while to figure it out, but I know now that it's time for me to make some changes."

"Changes?" asked Sarge. "What kind of changes?"

"It's pointless to resist change, man," said Fillmore.

"You're right, Fillmore," said Lightning.

"Really?" Fillmore said, a little surprised.

"Which is why I have an announcement to make," Lightning replied. Everyone tensed up, anxiously waiting for what Lightning had to say. "I've thought long and hard about it," he said. They all leaned in. "Done a lot of soul searching and considered all the options." They drew closer, crowding around him, afraid to miss a word. "And I've finally decided –"

"You do want to keep racing?" blurted Luigi, unable to contain his worry. He was clearly asking what everyone was thinking.

"Are you kidding?" said Lightning. "Of course I wanna keep racing!"

The crowd exhaled with relief, and then exploded into a chorus of hoots and hollers.

"Phew!" said Mater. "Oh, wait. Forgot I already knew that!"

"Guys," said Lightning. "I'm talking about making this my best season yet!"

Everyone cheered and jumped for joy.

"We were hoping you'd say that!" said Dusty.

Lightning waited until the crowd settled down and then spoke in a serious tone. "The thing is, guys, if I'm gonna beat Storm, I need to train like him."

"We're way ahead of you, buddy!" said Dusty.

"Lightning, we want you on the road first thing in the morning," said Rusty.

"Yeah," said Dusty. "So you can come out and see the brand-new …"

"… RUST-EZE RACING CENTRE!" Dusty and Rusty finished together.

"It's wicked awesome!" said Dusty.

"Wait – what?" said Lightning with a big smile. "Rust-eze Racing Centre?"

"It's got all the fancy bells and whistles that the kids are training on these days," said Dusty. "We'll send Macky boy the directions. Now get movin', all right?"

"Okay!" said Lightning, stunned.

The screen went black as they ended the call. And the gang erupted in an even louder celebration than before, feeling ecstatic and hopeful.

As Lightning and Sally drove out, Luigi and Guido scurried past. "Andiamo! Andiamo!" said Guido.

"Guido, come!" urged Luigi. "We have to pack the tyres!"

Ramone rolled up alongside Lightning. "Hey, Lightning!" he called. "You can't race in primer, man. Come on! Let's go." Lightning took off with Ramone.

He looked back at Sally and smiled as she proudly watched him go.

Moments later, Lightning was up on the lift in Ramone's garage. Ramone got to work, giving Lightning a fresh paint job. Once he was finished, Lightning checked himself out in the mirror, admiring his new look. "Ramone, you have done it again," he said.

"It's like the Sistine Chapel – on wheels," said Ramone.

Lightning stared at his reflection, a determined look in his eyes. "I'm coming for you, Storm," he said.

CHAPTER 7

As the sun rose over the spiralling red rocks of Radiator Springs, Mack's trailer was packed and ready to go. The gang surrounded Lightning, buzzing with excitement, admiring his new paint job.

"That's quite a spit-shine!" said Sarge.

"You look great, man!" said Fillmore.

Lightning turned to Sally before heading into the truck. "You look … different," said Sally.

"Obviously," Lightning said.

"You look ready," she said.

Luigi and Guido scooted over, ready to go. Guido was towing a huge trunk.

"Guido, come!" shouted Luigi. "Scusi, scusi. Tyres coming through."

As Lightning started up the trailer ramp, Lizzie drove by and slapped him on the back bumper, startling him.

"Go kick those rookies in the boot!" she said.

Sally laughed, and Lightning started to load up. But he stopped for a brief moment. "I'll see you guys in Florida!" he shouted to his friends.

They wished him luck and said their goodbyes.

"Don't forget to call me!" said Mater.

"Good luck in college!" Lizzie called. It was no secret that Lizzie had trouble keeping the year straight, but regardless of whether she knew why Lightning was leaving, she knew she was going to miss him.

Sally and Lightning shared a glance, filled with hope and gratitude. Before the trailer door dropped, Lightning said, "Hey, Sal. Thanks."

"Anytime," she replied.

"Rust-eze Racing Centre, here we come!" said Mack. "Good times ahead! Yeeeeah!"

The door closed and Mack drove away. He headed out of Radiator Springs and drove across the long stretch of road. They crossed mountains, passed through farmland and little towns, driving into the sunset and through the night. Soon after the sun rose the next morning, they arrived at Rust-eze Racing Centre.

Lightning stared at the impressive building, amazed by its modern look and sheer size. It was set back from the road and appeared to be made entirely of glass. The driveway looked like the turn of a racetrack, and the lines of the structure mimicked the flow of the grandstands at a speedway. The sun sparkled off its panels, making the whole place shimmer. It was spectacular. He couldn't wait to see what it looked like inside.

As Mack's trailer door lifted, Lightning rolled out to a mass of reporters. They barked his name along with a slew of questions.

"Hey, Lightning! Over here!" shouted one.

"Have you seen the latest records Storm's been setting?" shouted another.

"Have you given any thought to retirement? Lightning!"

Lightning's eyes narrowed as he squinted against the bright, popping flashbulbs of their cameras. Luigi and Guido darted out in front defensively. They covered him and tried to dissolve the crowd.

"Okay!" shouted Luigi. "That's enough. No questions! Scuzi. Out of the way! Coming through! Back up. Back up!"

But the reporters and photographers continued, shouting Lightning's name and snapping photos.

"No pictures!" ordered Luigi. "No, no, no. Hey! Back away. No, no, no, no!"

Once they had escorted Lightning through the sea of cameras and questions, the friends went inside the racing centre.

"Paparazzi!" shouted Guido. "Ptui!" He pretended to spit at them from behind the glass door.

No longer distracted by the reporters, Lightning, Luigi and Guido stood, dumbfounded, looking at the incredible training facility. A giant red sculpture of the number 95 stood in the centre of the massive lobby, and banners with 95 on them were hanging from the extremely high ceiling, reaching down towards the centre of the room.

"Oooooh! Wow!" said Lightning, impressed. There were even action shots from Lightning's career featured all over the freestanding display cases in the lobby.

Rusty and Dusty approached, beaming. "Whaddaya think?" Dusty asked.

"What do I think? It's unbelievable!" Lightning exclaimed. He continued looking around, taking it all in. "Guys, how did you ever do this?"

Dusty looked over at Rusty. "You want to tell him, or should I tell him?"

"Ah, you start!" said Rusty. "Go ahead, go ahead!"

"We sold Rust-eze!" Dusty exclaimed.

"What?" Lightning asked. He couldn't believe it.

"You think a couple of losers like us could do this on our own?" Dusty asked with a laugh.

"Wait," said Lightning. "You sold Rust-eze?"

"It's all good news," said Dusty. "We just realized you needed something that we couldn't give you. It felt like the time was right for us, too," he said with a smile. "I mean, we're not as young and handsome as we look."

"You ain't kiddin', man!" said Rusty, and they both laughed.

"Besides, this Sterling fella? He's got every high-tech thing you'll ever need," added Dusty.

"Whoa, whoa, whoa, Sterling? Who's Sterling?" asked Lightning.

"Lightning McQueen!" said a friendly voice. A stylish silver car smiled as he rolled down an enormous ramp, and welcomed Lightning to the centre. "You made some serious time, partner."

"He's the Mudflap King of the Eastern Seaboard!"

exclaimed Rusty. "And a big fan of yours!"

"Welcome to the Rust-eze Racing Centre," said Sterling. "You have no idea how much I've been looking forward to this."

"Thanks, uh … Mister …" Lightning said, still a bit shocked.

"Please. No 'Mister'. Just Sterling. I have been a fan of yours forever. And to be your sponsor? How great is that?" He looked over at Rusty and Dusty. "I can't thank Rusty and Dusty here enough." He leaned in and whispered, "Tough negotiators, by the way."

"Ah. You flatter us – but don't stop!" said Dusty. Then he and Rusty burst out laughing again.

"Anyway, just wanted to say a quick hello. Take as much time as you need," Sterling said. "Door's always open, guys," he added, looking at Rusty and Dusty. A forklift rolled over to him with a clipboard that needed Sterling's attention. He nodded to everyone, then slipped out.

Lightning, Rusty and Dusty made their way towards the door. They stopped, and Lightning stuttered, trying to find the right words to say. Even though he was excited about the new centre, he felt bad about having to say goodbye to them. "Well, I sure am gonna miss racing for you guys."

"Ya know, you gave us a lot of great memories, Lightning. Memories we'll remember," said Dusty.

"Well said," Rusty added.

They headed for the door, then looked back at

Lightning. "Oh, and whatever you do," said Rusty. "Don't drive like my brother."

"Don't drive like my brother!" added Dusty.

As Rusty and Dusty left the building, reporters swirled and surrounded them. "No, no, please," said Dusty. "No pictures. Okay, maybe one. Get my good side though, will ya?"

Lightning chuckled as he watched them go. Then he turned and looked around the centre, and something on one of the displays caught his eye. He went to take a closer look, and realized it was part of an even larger exhibition that stretched the length of the corridor.

Sterling appeared in the distance and came to him. "So? You like it?" he asked.

"Oh, hey, Mr Sterling. Wow! My career on a wall. Nice that you included Doc."

"Of course – he's your mentor," Sterling replied.

"Yeah," Lightning said. Then he noticed something else. On one of the shelves were some glass jars containing different kinds of dirt and asphalt with labels underneath. "Jars of dirt?" he asked.

"Sacred dirt," said Sterling. "Each of those jars contains dirt from all the old tracks that Doc raced on: Florida International, Thunder Hollow just down the road, and our very own Fireball Beach, right outside."

"Huh. Hey, is that –" Lightning said pointing to one of the jars.

"A bit of asphalt from Glen Ellen –"

"My first win!" Lightning exclaimed, tickled.

"You really are a fan."

"I am. And a fan of your future." Sterling looked Lightning in the eyes. "You ready for it?"

"Definitely," Lightning said. For the first time in months, he finally felt ready.

CHAPTER 8

Whoosh. Thump. Thump. A new body wrap was sealed snugly around Lightning. He wriggled uncomfortably as he tried to settle into the tight material.

"It's an electronic suit," said Sterling, noticing that Lightning seemed unsure. "With it we'll be able to track your speed and your vital signs."

"Really? Does it have a phone?" asked Lightning.

"Don't be crazy! Racing cars don't have phones!" said Sterling with a chuckle.

Moments later, Lightning was parked on an overlook, peering down on the training area of the racing centre. "This is really impressive," he said, eyeing all the fancy equipment below.

"Not bad, huh?" said Sterling. He led Lightning down to the lower floor, continuing the tour. "This centre is the most coveted destination for young racers training to make our team someday. And this is where you'll train until you leave for Florida." As they wheeled around the facility, Sterling listed a few of their amazing features. "Treadmills, wind tunnels, virtual reality ..."

They looked down as three racers wearing virtual reality goggles awkwardly bumped into each other. "Still working on that," Sterling said, then continued. "And the best fitness regimens anyone could possibly imagine –"

"Ho, ho, ho – is that the simulator?" Lightning asked, interrupting Sterling.

"Oh, yes. Lightning, I'd like to introduce you to the multimillion-dollar flagship of interactive race simulation," said Sterling.

Lightning was fascinated by the machine.

"The XDL 24 GTS Mark Z," Sterling said.

"The XDL 24 – GTS Mark Z," Lightning repeated. He marvelled at its mysterious beauty.

"Jackson Storm wishes he had this model," said Sterling.

Lightning was awestruck. The simulator sat on a platform above the floor, and Lightning couldn't wait to get a closer look. As he and Sterling drove up, Lightning noticed a yellow car on it, facing away. Three Next Gens idled nearby as they watched the car race. On the simulator screen, the chequered flag appeared, and the car crossed the finish line. The platform lowered and rotated, and the yellow car exited the simulator to cheers from the Next Gens.

"It's just like being on a real track," the yellow car said to the young cars. "So put your hours in. Okay! Let's hit the treadmills. Come on! Show me what you got!"

The car drove right past Lightning and Sterling, leading the Next Gens to the high-tech treadmills.

"Who's the racer?" Lightning asked.

"She's a trainer," Sterling replied. "Cruz Ramirez. Best trainer in the business."

Sterling and Lightning watched as the Next Gens climbed aboard the treadmills and started training. Lightning's eyes grew wide. He noticed that above each treadmill was a digital readout of the car's speed. They were all going between 270 to 290 kilometres per hour. Just then, Cruz jumped onto the leader's treadmill and began exercising with her students. Her treadmill had a panel that controlled the Next Gens' machines.

"Ready to meet it, greet it, and defeat it?" she shouted, like a drill sergeant.

The Next Gens cheered along with her.

"All right! Now bring up those RPMs!"

"Like the attitude!" Lightning whispered to Sterling.

"Yeah. We call her our Maestro of Motivation," Sterling replied.

"You're drivin' a little tense again, Ronald," said Cruz.

Ronald was riding ridiculously high and tense, but he tried to play it off. "No, no, no, I'm cool."

"Do your exercise," ordered Cruz. She hit a button, and a picture of a peaceful cloud against a blue sky appeared on Ronald's monitor.

"I am a fluffy cloud. I am a fluffy cloud. I am a fluffy cloud," Ronald repeated. He relaxed, and suddenly his speed increased.

"There ya go," said Cruz, pleased.

"You're a cloud," said the Next Gen beside Ronald, mocking him.

"Shut up, Kurt!" he shouted, tensing up again.

"Here come the bugs, Kurt. You ready?" said Cruz.

Kurt cringed, preparing himself. "Ready!"

Cruz pushed a button, and bugs blasted out of the front of Kurt's treadmill, pelting him. Once they stopped, he brightened. "Hey, I kept my eyes open this time!"

"Gotta see that track!" said Cruz.

"Oh, no," said Cruz, noticing Gabriel, a Next Gen who was staring off into space and driving at a much slower speed than the rest. "Homesick again, Gabriel?" she asked gently.

"Yes," he said.

Cruz hit a button, and modern Latin music blared out of Gabriel's treadmill. A picture of his hometown appeared on his monitor.

"Santa Cecilia! Mi ciudad!" he said.

"Use that! Win for them!" shouted Cruz.

Gabriel's speed increased, and the number on his monitor rapidly rose. "Gracias!"

"De nada!" Cruz replied.

"Wow!" Lightning said, impressed by both the cool technology and Cruz's effectiveness.

"She trains young racers to push through their own obstacles," explained Sterling. "Tailor-made for each one." He looked over at Lightning. "Now she's gonna work with you."

"And I don't wanna see a drop in those RPMs – DO NOT drop those RPMs!" Cruz shouted, completely focused on the racers.

Sterling called to Cruz, and he and Lightning joined her on the training room floor. She turned off the treadmills, and the racers took a break. "I'd like to introduce you to Lightning McQueen –"

"I hear you're the Maestro," said Lightning.

"Mr Sterling, did you say Lightning McQueen was here, because I don't see him anywhere," said Cruz. "He's obviously an imposter." She eyed Lightning up and down. "He looks old and broken-down, with flabby tyres!"

"Hey!" shouted Lightning defensively. "I do not!"

"Use that!" said Cruz.

"Whoa!" said Lightning, laughing. "Yeah, I see. I can use that energy for motivation. *Rarrrr.* Right."

"It's all about motivation, Mr McQueen," explained Cruz. "Indecision, anger, even fear – you can use anything negative as fuel to push through to the positive." Cruz smiled. "Oh, I am so excited that I get to train you. I grew up watching you on TV."

Lightning nodded.

"Those young guys are great and all, but I like a challenge!" said Cruz.

Lightning chuckled, trying not to feel insulted. "I'm not that much older, but ..." his voice trailed off.

"In fact, I call you my senior project," said Cruz, looking at him proudly.

Lightning blinked, unsure of how to respond. Now he was officially insulted.

CHAPTER 9

Pulsing, energetic Latin music pumped and thumped through an exercise studio as Cruz rocked to the dance beat. "We need to loosen those ancient joints," she said over the music, moving around as if leading an aerobics class for the elderly.

Lightning stood and watched her. He was confused at first; then he slowly started to join her in the exercises.

"First, the wheels!" she said to the beat. "And forward and rest, and forward, and rest. Join me! Rest...."

"Is all this resting necessary?" Lightning asked.

"We're working you in slowly," Cruz said. Then she continued chanting to the beat of the music. "And reach for your lunch. Reach for your lunch. Now reeeach to the front.... What is there? It's your luuuunch!"

Lightning rolled his eyes and followed her moves, slowly lifting and rotating each tyre, one at a time. He sighed. This was not the training he was anticipating.

"Now backwards!" Cruz said. "Is lunch there?"

"When do we go on the simulator?" Lightning asked, impatient.

Over the next few days, Cruz had Lightning perform a variety of exercises. At one point, she set him up in the centre of a table that resembled a see-saw. She leaned forward and said, "Good morning, Mr McQueen." Then she tilted the table at such a harsh angle, Lightning was almost entirely vertical. His rear tyres were suspended in the air, and as he stared downwards, his bonnet was centimetres from the ground. "Whoa," Lightning said, uncomfortable.

"Looking good!" Cruz said. Lightning asked her why she thought this was helpful. "This'll get oil to places it hasn't been in a long time," she explained. Then she slid a drip pan directly below him.

"Is that … a drip pan?" Lightning asked. He was horrified.

"Just in case!" Cruz chirped.

"How old do you think I am?"

Cruz didn't answer. "Visualize yourself driving fast down a steep hill," she said, trying to get him to focus. "I'll be back in a few." Then she literally left him hanging.

"Visualize? Wait, no!" Lightning called for her, but she rolled away. "A few what?" he shouted.

Once he realized that she wasn't coming back anytime soon, he sighed and settled himself in a position. "I just want to go on the simulator," he said to himself.

Just then, Kurt, one of the next-gen racers he'd seen earlier, drove through. "How's it hanging, Drip Pan?" he mocked.

A little while later, Cruz put Lightning on the treadmill. At one point he looked over at Kurt on a nearby machine and noticed that Kurt was moving much faster than him.

"'Sup," said Kurt.

Cruz came over to check Lightning's progress. "I've set a maximum speed to conserve your energy," said Cruz. "What I want you to do is visualize beating – this guy." She pushed a button, and a picture of Jackson Storm appeared on the monitor in front of Lightning.

"Storm?"

"Uh-huh. That's right! Get him! Get him, Mr McQueen!"

"Get him?" Lightning said. "This thing's only going like five miles an hour!"

"We'll work up to the higher speeds right after you take your nap," said Cruz.

"Nap? I don't need a nap," Lightning was irritated.

The Next Gens chuckled amongst themselves, laughing at Lightning's expense.

"I am not taking a nap!" said Lightning.

Later that day, wind chimes jingled and clinked as Cruz sat and meditated. Lightning opened his eyes with a yawn.

"How was your nap, Mr McQueen?" she asked.

"It was kinda ... refreshing, actually," he said. Then he noticed a strange scent wafting through the air. "What's that burning-rubber smell?" He looked over and saw incense sticks with little billows of smoke curling towards the ceiling. Suddenly, some pitties entered and gently removed Lightning's tyres. "Oh! Hey!" he shouted.

"You've been driving on tyres a long time," said Cruz. "Have you ever stopped to get to know them?"

"I'm sorry, what?"

"Tyres are individuals. You should give each one a name."

"Name them?" said Lightning, flabbergasted. "No. I'm not doing that."

"Mine are named Maria, Juanita, Ronaldo, and Debbie Richardson."

"What?"

"Long story."

"May I have my tyres back so I can go to the simulator, please?" asked Lightning.

"Name them!" ordered Cruz.

"Okay. Uh, Lefty, Righty, Backy and Backy Jr."

"Does this make you mad?" asked Cruz.

"Yes it does!"

"Use that!"

Later on, the dance music blared again. "And merge and yield and merge and yield," Cruz chanted with the beat and honked her horn to the rhythm. "Now you got some tyre damage...."

Lightning rolled his eyes, then noticed one of the young racers getting off the simulator.

"Speed bump. Speed bump," continued Cruz. "Now clean up your messy garage. Bug in the windscreen. Bug in the windscreen."

"Thank you, Cruz. I'm done," said Lightning.

"Mr McQueen!" Cruz exclaimed. "Where're you going?"

Lightning sped straight to the simulator. "To the future!" he shouted.

Cruz caught up to him while he was fiddling with the knobs and buttons, trying to turn it on. "Okay! Here we go," Lightning said. "How do I do this? Come on, baby!"

"Mr McQueen," Cruz warned.

"Cruz, thank you for the old-man training – as crazy as it was – but I'm warmed up enough and now I need you to launch this thing."

"Mr McQueen, wait until you can handle it. Please? There are no shortcuts."

But Lightning refused to get off the machine. Suddenly, Sterling appeared on the balcony above. "All right!" he said excitedly. "My star racer is on the simulator!"

"Why, yes, I am!" said Lightning, beaming.

"Well, let's see you take it out for a spin," said Sterling.

"Right away, Mr Sterling, owner of the company," Lightning said, eyeing Cruz.

Cruz shook her head and fired up the simulator. "Okay. Have fun," she said.

Finally, the simulator whizzed to life. It raised Lightning up and a wall-sized screen appeared in front of him. "This is what I'm talkin' about!" he said, feeling confident. Then, out of nowhere, magnetic wheel guards zipped out, rotated up, and were secured around his tyres. "Oooh, didn't know about those," he said.

"Prepare to race," said the simulator's monotone mechanical voice. "The green flag is out."

"What did it say? Is it talking?" said Lightning. "I don't see the flag. What do I do?"

"Go!" shouted Cruz.

"Go?" asked Lightning

"Go!" Cruz repeated.

The simulator began to move, and Lightning felt uneasy as he tried to balance and use the machine correctly. "Okay. This isn't so bad." But he definitely didn't have the hang of it. "Whoa! Huh, that's sensitive. Okay . . . ah!"

"You have hit a wall," said the simulator.

"It shouldn't be this hard! Should it? Ah!" Lightning screamed. Then he hit the wall again. "You're fighting the simulator. Just race like you always do!" said Cruz.

But he continued to hit the wall – and the simulator announced it every time.

"Whoa. There can't be this many walls on a regular track!" he yelled.

Soon a car nudged by Lightning and yelled, "Hey! Watch it, buddy!"

"You have been passed by Jackson Storm," said the simulator.

"Wait! Storm's in here?"

"For motivation! Get your speed up!" shouted Cruz.

"I am trying!" cried Lightning.

"Storm races at 207," said Cruz. "You're at 195. Pick it up, Mr McQueen!"

Lightning pushed himself and grunted as he tried to move faster. The simulator swayed and shimmied. Cruz looked up at Sterling and saw the concern on his face. She focused back on Lightning and tried to help him, but he screamed as he hit another wall.

"Mr McQueen," said Cruz, "come down from there and we'll work you up to this."

He looked away from the screen to talk to Cruz. "I am fine, Cruz! I can do it, okay?" But that was a mistake. He careened through the virtual pit area, and everything erupted into chaos. "Whoa!"

"You have jumped a barrier," said the simulator, reporting every mistake. "You have maimed two vehicles. You have destroyed a drinking fountain."

Animated ambulances and fire engines appeared on the screen and moved into the scene. Lightning screamed, but he was unable to straighten out and escape the mayhem.

"You have destroyed a building," said the simulator. "You have disabled an ambulance." Things kept getting worse! "You are on fire."

Then he could hear the deafening sound of a screaming, panicked crowd as the simulator continued to report the damage. "You are on fire. Danger. Danger. Crash imminent." Lightning tried to get back on the track, but the chaos continued. He was completely out of control. "You are going the wrong way," said the simulator.

"Look out!" shouted Lightning.

"Turn back. Turn back," repeated the simulator.

Out of ideas, Lightning tried to free himself from

the simulator's magnetic wheel restraints. He struggled, attempting to get loose, but the simulator threw him forward.

"Turn it off! Turn it off!" yelled Lightning. "Get these things off me! *Whoooooooooaa!*"

Completely panicked and using sheer strength, Lightning finally freed himself. Nuts, bolts and screws broke off and fell from the simulator. Then he revved his engine, anxious to get off the platform.

But without the wheel restraints, Lightning actually crashed through the simulator's screen!

Cruz rolled up to him. "Are you all right?" she asked.

"You have crashed," repeated the simulator.

"I have crashed," moaned Lightning.

Sparks flew out of the simulator, and the room's lights flickered. Then the entire racing facility lost power.

CHAPTER 10

Destroying the multimillion-dollar simulator was not Lightning's proudest moment. He waited by the door to Sterling's office, sheepishly listening to the muffled voices of Sterling and Cruz. He tried to decipher what they were saying as they went back and forth inside Sterling's office. While Lightning eavesdropped, he stared at a forklift mopping the floor nearby.

"It's not easy for him," said Cruz. "Are you sure? Give him another chance. I can still work with him.... Can't you just...? We still have time."

"Cruz, just relax. I will. I will talk to him. I know he's your project. Yes. Cruz, let me handle this my way. Thank you," said Sterling.

The forklift looked up at Lightning. "You're all washed up, McQueen!" she said.

Lightning did a double take. "I'm sorry. What did you say?"

"Said the floor's all washed up and clean!"

"Oh, right," said Lightning.

Cruz exited Sterling's office and quietly moved over to

Lightning. "Good luck," she whispered.

Lightning looked at Cruz, then rolled towards Sterling. "C'mon in!" said Sterling in a big, welcoming voice. "Got somethin' to show ya." He smiled as he took a breath. "You ready?"

"Ah, for what?" asked Lightning. He rolled into Sterling's office and saw an amazing array of items – movie posters, advertisements, giant cardboard displays – all with Lightning's image on them. "Wow."

"You are about to become the biggest brand in racing," said Sterling. "Movie deals, product endorsements...." Sterling's voice trailed off as he let the information sink in.

Lightning looked around. "Mud flaps," he said, noticing a set of them on the wall.

"Of course. We'll be rich beyond belief. You think you're famous now?" Sterling said with a laugh.

"I thought you'd be mad about the simulator," said Lightning. "This is all great, Mr Sterling, I guess, but I don't know. I've never really thought of myself as a brand."

"Oh, nor do I," said Sterling. "I'm a fan. Maybe your most avid. I think of this as your legacy."

"Hey," said Lightning, concern creeping into his voice. "That sounds like something that happens after you're … done racing."

Sterling didn't respond. He lowered his gaze.

"Mr Sterling, what is this about?" Lightning asked.

Sterling sighed and broke the news. "Look, Lightning. I'm not gonna race you."

Lightning couldn't believe what he was hearing.

He immediately asked Sterling to explain.

"Hold on, hold on," said Sterling, trying to calm Lightning down.

"I'm not going to Florida?"

"Lightning, you have no idea how excited I was to get you here, because I knew, I knew you'd be back. It was gonna be the comeback story of the year! But your speed and performance just aren't where they need to be. I'm sorry." He turned away and headed over to the window that overlooked the training room.

"We're talking about speed on the simulator," said Lightning. "Listen to how crazy that sounds!"

"Look, I'm trying to help you," said Sterling. "As your sponsor, yes, but also as your friend. Your racing days are coming to an end. Every time you lose, you damage yourself."

"Damage the brand, you mean," Lightning said bitterly.

"Oh, Lightning, come on," said Sterling, turning to face him. "You've done the work. Now move on to the next phase and reap the reward."

"The racing is the reward. Not the stuff," said Lightning. "I don't want to cash in. I want to feel the rush of moving two hundred miles an hour, inches from the other guys, pushing myself faster than I thought I could go! That's the reward, Mr Sterling."

But Sterling wasn't budging.

"Look," said Lightning. "I can do this. I can, I promise! I'll train like I did with Doc! I'll get my tyres dirty on every dirt track from here to Florida." Lightning gestured out of the window. "I can start right there on Fireball Beach, where all the old greats used to race!"

"Get your tyres dirty," said Sterling. "That's how you're gonna beat Storm?"

"Yes! Exactly!" said Lightning. "I mean, sacred dirt, right? Mr Sterling, if you care about my legacy – the one that Doc started – you'll let me do this. I promise you, I will win!"

"I don't know. What you're asking … it's too risky."

"C'monnnnn," said Lightning with a twinkle in his eye. "You like it, I can tell. It's got that little comeback-story-of-the-year feel to it, doesn't it?"

Sterling stared at Lightning for a moment. He was running the idea through his mind, turning it over and over. Finally, he said, "One race?"

Lightning grinned.

"If you don't win in Florida, you'll retire?"

"Look, if I don't win, I'll sell all the mud flaps ya got!" said Lightning. "But if I do win, I decide when I'm done. Deal?"

Sterling paused for a long time. "Deal," he said.

"Thank you, Mr Sterling!" Lightning replied. "You won't be sorry."

"Just one thing," said Sterling. "And this is only because I don't like taking chances. You're taking someone with you."

CHAPTER 11

The waves rolled up onto the shore of Fireball Beach as Cruz awkwardly dragged a high-tech crash trolley across the sand dunes.

"Way to go, Mr McQueen!" she yelled, struggling as she tried to manoeuvre the equipment through the soft sand.

Lightning sighed as he watched Cruz. He couldn't believe she was the one Sterling had wanted to send with him. Luigi and Guido stood beside him, looking equally surprised.

"You talked him into it!" exclaimed Cruz. She was excited, but also extremely out of breath from struggling with the trolley. "Man, you could talk a – snowmobile – into buying an air conditioner."

"You are going with me? With that thing?" asked Lightning.

"Yeah! You still need my help, Mr McQueen. You're brittle ... like a fossil," Cruz said, settling the cart into place. She fiddled with the buttons and knobs for a moment and, suddenly, a treadmill folded out.

"I don't need a trainer out here, Cruz," said Lightning.

"You're old. What if you fall on this beach and can't get up?" she retorted.

"Well, life's a beach … and then you drive," Lightning said. He looked over at Luigi and Guido, who both laughed at his joke.

"It's nice out here," Cruz said as she made some final adjustments to the equipment. "I can see why Mr Sterling said you wanted to train on the beach." The machine beeped. "Okay! We're all booted up. Just climb on the treadmill and I'll track your speed."

Lightning looked at her with disbelief. "What?" he shouted. "No! The whole idea is getting my tyres dirty on the beach – the origin of racing. Real racing! I'm not drivin' on that thing when I've got the sand – and the whole Earth!"

"Oh. Okay," said Cruz. She turned off the machine and it wound down.

"Luigi! Let's do this thing!" shouted Lightning.

Lightning stood at the starting line, and Luigi positioned himself as the starter. "Welcome, racers, to Fireball Beach!" said Luigi. "Historic home for today's great test of speed. Our finish line will be the abandoned pier in the distance!" He gestured towards an old wooden pier about a kilometre down the beach.

Readying himself, Lightning twisted his tyres, forcing them to sink slightly into the sand. Cruz watched curiously as Lightning prepared.

"All right," he whispered. He took a deep breath to

settle himself, enjoying the soft sand beneath his tyres. "Quicker than quick, faster than fast, I am speed...."

"That is great self-motivation," said Cruz, interrupting his ritual. "Did you come up with that?"

Lightning smiled. "Yeah, I did."

"On your mark!" Luigi shouted.

"Note to self – more of that!" said Cruz.

"Get set! Goooooo!" Luigi shouted.

Lightning gunned it. He sped along the beach, rushing through the salty air until he sailed beneath the pier. He skidded to a stop, cheering, "*Whoooo-hooo*! There ya go! Felt good!" He turned towards Cruz and shouted, "Hey! What was my speed?"

"I don't know," Cruz called back.

"What?" he exclaimed.

"I can only track you on the treadmill!"

Lightning's face fell. He hadn't thought of that. He rolled back to the starting line. "No treadmills. But I do need to be able to track my speed," he said, thinking about what to do next.

Cruz sighed. Then she brightened. "Oooh! I know! Hamilton!"

"Hamilton here," said a computerized voice.

"Who's Hamilton?" asked Lightning.

"My electronic personal assistant," replied Cruz. "Hamilton, track Mr McQueen's speed and report it."

"Tracking," said Hamilton.

"Your suit will transmit your speeds to Hamilton. I'll stay as close as I can, 'cause this thing has a crazy-short range," explained Cruz.

"Fine. Whatever. Let's do this!" said Lightning. He rushed through his preparation: "Quicker than quick, faster than fast, I am speed. Come on, Luigi!"

"On your mark! Get set! Go!" shouted Luigi.

Lightning gunned it, and Hamilton called out Lightning's speed. "46 miles per hour … 63 miles per hour …" the computerized voice said. Then suddenly, a loud beeping noise blared, and Hamilton said, "Out of range."

Cruz was still at the starting line, her wheels spinning and sinking in the sand. "Huh," she said to herself. "That's odd."

When Lightning realized Cruz wasn't with him, he turned to see her stuck.

"I didn't go!" Cruz called.

Lightning headed back. "On sand, you gotta ease into your start so your tyres can grab. Okay?" said Lightning.

"Okay," answered Cruz.

"All right, let's go again!" Lightning shouted as he set himself to race.

"Go!" shouted Luigi.

The two took off, and Hamilton tracked Lightning's speed. "54 miles per hour … 65 miles per hour...."

Hamilton made a loud beeping noise again and said, "Out of range."

Lightning turned back to see Cruz off course, this time stuck in softer sand.

"Sorry," called Cruz. "Got stuck!"

"Go again!" shouted Lightning.

Luigi paused for a moment before yelling, "Go!"

Lightning raced off with Cruz beside him, but this time she ended up in the shallow waves. "Sorry!" she shouted as the water lapped around her.

Once they were back at the starting line, Luigi called for them to race again. But Cruz completely lost control, spinning doughnuts in the sand.

They tried again, and she ended up half buried.

"The beach ate me," she said. She kicked up and sprayed sand everywhere as she spun her tyres, trying to get out.

Luigi called them to their marks once again, and Lightning, irritated, tried to give Cruz a quick briefing.

"All right, Cruz. Pick a line on the compacted sand. You gotta have traction, or you're gonna spin out. Let's do this thing!"

"Get set. Go!" said Luigi.

They took off, and Hamilton read out Lightning's mileage. "122 … 134.…"

BEEP BEEP BEEP.

"Out of range," said Hamilton.

Lightning turned back and saw Cruz stopped on the beach again. But this time she wasn't stuck. She looked like she was just … waiting.

"Now what?" shouted Lightning.

"I didn't want to hit a crab," said Cruz.

"You gotta be kidding me!"

"What? It was cute."

Lightning screamed in frustration and looked up at

the sky, noticing the setting sun. He hurried back to the starting line, ready to race once again.

"All right," said Lightning, exhausted and annoyed. "One last chance to try this before it gets dark." He turned to Cruz. "Now, you're gonna take off slow to let your tyres grab."

"Yes," said Cruz.

"And pick a straight line on hard sand so you don't spin out."

"Uh-huh."

"And all of the crabbies have gone night-night –"

"Mr McQueen?"

"All right. Let's go again."

"And go!" shouted Luigi.

They took off racing along the same stretch of beach, this time under a pink sky. Cruz managed to keep up and not spin out, so Hamilton was able to track Lightning's speed. "155 miles per hour … 175 …" said Hamilton.

Lightning crossed under the old pier, winded but elated. "*Whooo-hoooo*! All right, finally! You made it. Congratulations! How'd I do?" he asked.

"You topped out at 198," said Cruz.

"One ninety eight that's it?"

"Still slower than Storm," said Cruz.

The two quietly headed back to the truck. They rolled over a dune towards Mack. Lightning sighed. "Wasted my whole day," he muttered.

"I wouldn't say that. It did feel great to be out here with the wind in our faces, doing real racing!" said

Cruz, upbeat. She felt completely energized after dashing against the ocean breeze.

"This isn't real racing! We're on a beach! All you do is go straight. How is that gonna prove anything?" Lightning's eyes were drawn to a sign on the side of the road: Sparks Ridge 46 miles. Thunder Hollow 72 miles. He moved closer to the sign, and Cruz followed.

"Thunder Hollow," Lightning said. "There's a dirt track there. That's what I need – to race against actual racers."

Luigi and Guido came over. "No!" shouted Luigi. "Too public. As the head of security, I must forbid it! If the press finds you, they will be like many, many bugs on you!"

"Paparazzi!" said Guido, disgusted. He spat on the ground.

"I really need this, guys," said Lightning.

"Leave it to me, boss," said Mack. Then he put on his best spy voice and said, "I am a master of disguise."

CHAPTER 12

The night sky was full of beautiful stars, but it was hard to see them under the bright spotlights of Thunder Hollow Speedway. Masses of locals tailgated in the Speedway's car park, while others made their way into the small-town stadium.

Just outside the entrance, tucked out of sight, Mack's disguised trailer waited. Instead of his normal flashy red-and-yellow paint job, Mack now sported an advertisement for Jocko Flocko's Party Supplies on the side of his trailer. Behind Mack, Guido watched as Luigi spun his tyres in mud, splattering it onto Lightning to hide his identity. Once he was finished, Lightning coughed and spat out bits of gunk that had flown into his mouth.

"You, sir, are officially incognito," said Mack. "Nobody's bothering you."

"The great Lightning McQueen," said Luigi, shaking his head.

"Well, at least it's official Thunder Hollow Speedway mud. It's sacred!" said Lightning.

Guido finished disguising Lightning by scraping away

some of the mud along his side, turning his number 95 into a 15.

The track announcer's voice was loud over the PA. "Racers, get on over to the startin' line! *Puhhhronto*!" he said.

"All right, that's me," said Lightning, heading towards the track. As he approached the starting line, he could barely make it out. The dimly lit racetrack looked mysterious against the bright lights in the parking lot. Lightning thought it was odd but shook it off, excited and ready to race. "All right! Let's get some dirt on these tyres," he said.

An official named Roscoe rolled up to him. "Hey, now!" said Roscoe. "You that out-of-towner?"

"Uh, yes!" said Lightning. "That's me. Chester Whipplefilter."

Just then, Cruz rolled up to the starting line. "And I'm … Frances Beltline."

Lightning tried to hide it, but he was shocked to see her. "Cruz?" he whispered. "What are you doing?"

"I'm your trainer," said Cruz. "Gonna track your speed from the infield, Whipplefilter."

"Fine," muttered Lightning. "Just stay out of the way."

Lightning looked over at Roscoe, a little impatient. "Excuse me, sir. Where is everybody?"

"They'll be along," said Roscoe rather dubiously. "We always let our guests start right up front." He smiled and then quickly darted off.

Suddenly, loud music began to play throughout the

stadium, and the roar of the crowd swelled in anticipation. Other racers approached from behind Lightning and Cruz, and the sounds of the music and crowd continued to build.

An announcer's voice boomed through the PA speaker: "Welcome, y'all, to Thunder Hollow Speedway for tonight's edition of CURRRRAAAZY EIGHT!" He punched a button in his booth, and explosives blew in succession from stacked tyres that had been placed around the track. *KABOOM*! The display ended with one gigantic blast, revealing a demolition derby course shaped like a figure eight and made of dirt and mud.

As the smoke cleared, shards of tyre rubber rained down on Lightning and Cruz. A flaming tyre rolled by, and Lightning looked over at Cruz, suddenly not feeling so great. "Did he say Crazy Eight?" Lightning asked.

The announcer continued, "All right, race fans! You know what time it is! Introducing tonight's challengers."

A variety of rough-looking vehicles rolled out. There were beaten and battered trucks, cars and buses – each one covered in dents and scratches. They were spray-painted, welded and patched together in a way that made them look like the exact opposite of crisp, clean racing cars.

"*Wee-oo, wee-oo, wee-oo, we-oo!*" squealed Dr Damage, imitating a siren. He was a bashed-up ambulance with 'Rambulance' spray-painted along his side.

"Have a nice trip!" said Arvy, a dented RV (recreational vehicle) with big black circles around his eyes and a horseshoe hanging off his grille like a nose ring.

An old, battered police car laughed maniacally. "Protect and swerve!" he shouted, manoeuvring haphazardly across the dirt.

All the Crazy Eight racers roared and cackled as Cruz and Lightning looked on, horrified.

"Cruz," Lightning whispered. "This isn't what I thought it was. Come on – follow me and we'll slip out." They turned to escape the demolition derby, but the gate was slammed shut and locked before they could make a break for it. There was no escape!

"Rule number one," said Roscoe. "The gate closes? You race."

Cruz gasped as a pittie quickly sprayed a sloppy 20 on her sides.

"Rule number two," Roscoe continued. "Last car standing wins. Rule number three. No cursing – it's Family Night!"

"Excuse me, sir," Lightning started.

"I'm not even supposed to be out here!" yelled Cruz, frightened.

Just then, a battered car drove by, honking loudly, startling them both. They jumped and turned around to see the racer laughing a few centimetres away. "*Whoooooooooo*!" the racer said.

"And make way for the undefeated Crazy Eight champion, the Diva of Demolition, Miss Fritter!" said the announcer.

The crowd went wild as a yellow school bus thundered over, causing Lightning to scream.

LIGHTNING MCQUEEN

Lightning McQueen has years of racing experience, seven Piston Cup wins, and an undying passion for motorsports.

Skill, focus, hard work and sportsmanship are the pillars of Lightning McQueen's success. A success that his late, great mentor Doc Hudson helped build. Lightning's racing career is riding high until the new generation of blazing racers appear on the track. With the help of old friends and new, Lightning must prove he is far from done with racing!

⫽ACKSON STORM

Jackson Storm is part of the new generation of elite racers. He is skilled, focused, cool and seemingly unbeatable. Storm doesn't waste his time with the history of the sport. He's not there to make friends or be anyone's hero; he's there to win and he knows that every fraction of every second counts. The sport is changing and sleek Storm is the face of that change.

CRUZ RAMIREZ

A smart, young technician, Cruz Ramirez is hired to be Lightning McQueen's trainer on the high-tech racing simulators. She is competent and data driven, and like others of her generation, she believes completely in the power of technology. However, while she's fast on the simulators, she still has plenty to learn about the reality of racing itself. Luckily she learns fast, soaking up as much as she can from the world around her, especially from Lightning McQueen. She's had her share of rejection and failure, and now she is ready to do whatever it takes to succeed.

VROOM

On race day in Arizona, Jackson Storm overtakes Lightning McQueen and wins the race!

Back in Radiator Springs in Doc's garage, Lightning felt sad as he overheard the radio crackle: "It's safe to say that Lightning McQueen's racing days are over."

At the brand-new Rust-eze Racing Centre, Lightning spotted Cruz Ramirez – the best trainer in the business. Cruz was going to be Lightning's new trainer. If anyone could help Lightning win races again, it was Cruz Ramirez!

Cruz followed Lightning to Fireball Beach to track his speed. Lightning wished that Doc Hudson was around to help.

Lightning had an idea – Doc might not be around anymore, but the car who coached him was. Lightning had to find Doc's old trainer – Smokey.

In Thomasville, Smokey introduced Lightning and Cruz to his friends: three racing legends who had competed with Doc.

Smokey told a story about a famous race, where Doc had flipped over the top of another racer to take the victory!

Smokey trained Lightning and Cruz hard. However, in their last practice before the big race, Cruz overtook Lightning. Lightning *still* wasn't fast enough!

On the day of the Florida 500 race, Lightning told his team to work on Cruz instead of him. The crowd gasped when they saw Cruz join the race wearing Lightning's number.

With one lap to go, Cruz drew up alongside Storm. Remembering Doc's move, Cruz flipped up and over Storm and landed on the track.

VROOom

The crowd went wild as Cruz crossed the line for her first Piston Cup victory. Lightning couldn't have been more proud of his teammate and friend.

"Boo," said Miss Fritter in a low, raspy voice. She had two huge metal pipes that looked like horns on either side of her face, and a string of number plates hung up along a chain-link fence attached to her sides. "Lookie here, boys! We got us a couple rookies. I'm gonna call you Muddy Britches," she said, gesturing towards the disguised Lightning. "And you" – she gestured towards Cruz – "Lemonade."

"Hey! Neither one of them has a single dent!" said Arvy.

"Oh, I'm gonna fix that!" said Miss Fritter with a cackle.

The crowd chanted along with the announcer: "All right, everybody! Let's … go … RACIN'!"

Lightning and Cruz were plunged into absolute chaos. Crazy Eight racers came at them from every direction, slamming into each other along the way. Cruz pulled over and tried to hide behind a stack of tyres, and Lightning shouted, "Cruz, what are you doing? Gotta keep moving!"

"I shouldn't be out here!" said Cruz, trembling.

"Move, Cruz! Move!" Lightning pushed her out of her hiding place just in time – a racer immediately smashed into the stack of tyres.

Lightning rode alongside her and they managed to make it through the first lap unharmed. They slalomed through the danger while the other racers crashed into each other, hooting and hollering.

Cruz struggled while trying to make it around a sharp curve. She called back to Lightning, begging for help. "What do I do?" she yelled. "I can't steer!"

"Turn right to go left!" shouted Lightning. He wanted to teach her how to drift. "Turn right to go left!"

"That doesn't make any sense!" yelled Cruz. She wasn't getting it.

"Turn right to go left!" he repeated.

Racers continued to smash into each other. Dr Damage hit one of them so hard, he flew through the air. "*Whoohoo!*" shouted the racer cheerfully. Dr Damage laughed.

Then Miss Fritter pushed a pile of racers and a taxi in front of her, pinning Lightning up against another car. She chuckled as she pushed them all forward, enjoying every second of her destruction.

Another racer smashed into Miss Fritter's pile, and Lightning managed to break free. He and Cruz continued to navigate around the crazy demolition racers, terrified.

The taxi rammed into Arvy. "*Yahooooooo!*" screeched Arvy, laughing as he plunged towards the fence.

An old pizza delivery van smashed into the taxi, and Arvy laughed. A racer flew up into the air and spun upside down, screaming, "*Whooo-hooo!*"

"Look at my new hat!" Arvy said as the car landed right on top of his head.

Another racer got hit so hard, he flipped and spun towards the crowd. "I'm flyinnnnnnnn'!" he yelled. Then he plunged downwards. "No! I'm not flyin'!" He hit the gate, and one of his souped-up rockets broke off and sailed into the crowd.

"I got it!" yelled a fan, holding up the broken accessory. Everyone cheered!

"Turn right to go left. Turn right to go …" Cruz chanted, trying to steer safely through the course and stay out of everyone's way. But she continued to get pushed around, and she felt overwhelmed by the chaos around her. Panicking, she froze in the centre of the track, closed her eyes, and began to hyperventilate.

Miss Fritter set her sights on a taco truck. "Here I come, boy!"

"No!" screamed the truck. "No, no, no, no!"

Miss Fritter revved her engine and smashed into him so hard, he flipped into the air and smashed down with a loud boom!

Then Miss Fritter narrowed her eyes and smiled at the helpless Cruz. She began to charge towards her.

"Oh, no!" shouted Cruz.

"Buckle up, everybody!" said the announcer. "Because it's time for her to meet the…." He hit a button in the booth, and a banner unfurled. It read FRITTER END.

The crowd cheered along with the announcer. "FRITTER END!" they screamed. Flaming tyres exploded in front of the banner, adding to the dramatic moment.

As everyone in the crowd chanted, a worn-out fire engine named Mr Drippy shouted from the stands, "We love you, Miss Fritter!"

Miss Fritter took a lap, circling Cruz. "Your number plate's gonna look real nice in my collection," she said.

A nearby racer who had been flipped onto his roof offered a piece of advice to Cruz: "Run!"

Lightning was across the track, at the other end of the figure eight. He could see Miss Fritter preparing to ram Cruz. He had to do something.

"Don't fight it, Lemon. It'll only get worse for ya," said Miss Fritter. All of a sudden, a razor-sharp stop sign popped out of one of her sides, ready to rip into Cruz! Miss Fritter screamed and started her attack.

The crowd chanted "Fritter Time!" as she charged.

Just then, Lightning came to the rescue! He pushed Cruz out of harm's way seconds before Miss Fritter reached her. Miss Fritter watched as Lightning moved them off course, but her momentum was so strong, she couldn't stop. She sped right past Cruz and Lightning, swerving and skidding out of control! Cruz drove to safety, and Miss Fritter toppled over sideways in the mud.

"Oh, my gracious! Miss Fritter's down!" said the announcer.

The crowd shouted, "Ohhhh!"

"You gonna get it now, Whipplefilter!" called a fan from the stands.

While Lightning watched Miss Fritter's wreck, his tyres began to sink into the mud. He'd stayed still for too long. As he struggled to free himself, he saw that he had a sliced tyre. Miss Fritter's sharp stop sign must've nicked him when he pushed Cruz out of the way! Now he was stranded in the middle of the track.

Miss Fritter eyed Lightning as she tried to get off her side.

The crowd chanted, "Frit-ter! Frit-ter! Frit-ter!"

CHAPTER 13

Mack's horn blared as he hightailed it from Thunder Hollow. Inside the trailer, Cruz sat next to her gaudy Crazy Eight trophy. It was hideous. She was trying to hide her giddiness over winning her first race, but it was clear she was excited.

They heard a local reporter's voice coming from the television. "Fans here at Thunder Hollow are still buzzing over tonight's unexpected appearance of Lightning McQueen! Sharing the Crazy Eight track with local legend, Miss Fritter!"

Cruz and Lightning couldn't help watching.

"Oh, he's always been my favourite!" said Miss Fritter in her interview. "My garage is covered from head to toe with '95' posters."

Later on, Lightning stared off as Cruz rattled on about her ridiculous trophy.

"So …" said Cruz, "my trophy's kinda nice. Don't ya think?"

Lightning didn't say a word.

"I mean, I know you've got like a billion of them, so you

would know ..." Cruz lowered her gaze and mumbled to herself. "I still can't believe I won." She rambled on while Lightning remained quiet. "Looks like they spent a lot of money on it. I mean, I think it's real metal! It's pretty nice and shiny. I have never seen one up close. Actually, it seems pretty snazzy, considering it was such a small track, and –"

"Stop," said Lightning, finally breaking the silence. "Just ... just stop, okay, Cruz? You don't even know ... you don't even have one clue."

"Hey!" said Cruz. "I was just trying to –"

Luigi and Guido peered in from the loft, concerned.

"Do you know what happens if I lose this race?" asked Lightning. Cruz sat quietly. "Every mile of this trip was to get me faster than Jackson Storm. Faster! I started off getting nowhere for a WEEK on a simulator! I lose a whole day with you on Fireball Beach! And then I waste tonight in the crosshairs of Miss Fritter! I'm stuck at the same speed I was a month ago! I can't get any faster because I'm too busy taking care of my trainer!" Lightning took a pause, seething. Cruz was too startled to reply. "This is my last chance, Cruz. Last! Final! Finito! If I lose, I never get to do this again. If you were a racer, you'd know what I'm talking about. But you're not! So you don't!"

Lightning slammed his front tyre down in frustration, and the force knocked the trophy over, causing it to crack and crumble. Cruz gasped and thumped a button, calling for Mack on the trailer's intercom. "Pull over!" she shouted.

"Huh? Now?" asked Mack.

"Now!" said Cruz.

"Ahhh! Okay, okay. Pulling over!" said Mack.

Once he had stopped, Cruz stormed out of the trailer. Lightning followed. He wasn't sure where she was going or what she was doing.

"Ask me if I've dreamed of being a trainer, Mr McQueen! Go ahead!" said Cruz, lit with anger.

"Uhhh … I–I …" Lightning stammered, stunned by her fury.

"Ask me if I got up in the dark to run laps before school every day. Ask me if I saved every penny to buy a ticket to the races when they came to town. Ask me if I did that so that I could become a trainer someday. Ask me!"

Lightning fearfully complied. "Did y–"

"No!" Cruz shouted, cutting him off. "I've wanted to become a racer forever! Because of you!" She turned and started to slowly drive away. Lightning watched her briefly and moved closer, trying to think of a response.

"I used to watch you on TV, flying through the air.… You seemed so … fearless."

Lightning stayed quiet. He remembered those days with great fondness.

"'Dream small, Cruz.' That's what my family used to say. 'Dream small or not at all.'" Cruz took a minute before she continued. "They were just trying to protect me – but I was the fastest kid in town. And I was gonna prove them wrong!"

"What happened?" Lightning asked.

"When I got to my first race, I figured it out,"

Cruz replied proudly.

"What?"

"That I didn't belong," Cruz answered. "The other racers looked nothing like me. They were bigger and stronger and so ... confident, you know? And when they started their engines, I knew I could never compete. I just left. It was my one shot, and I didn't take it." Cruz sighed. "Yeah ... so, I'm gonna head back to the training centre. I think we both know it's for the best." She started to leave, then turned back to Lightning. "But can I ask you something?"

"Of course," he said.

"What was it like for you? When you showed up to your first race. How did you know you could do it?"

"I don't know," said Lightning. "I guess I just never thought that I couldn't."

"Huh," said Cruz. "I wish I knew what that felt like." Then she rolled away.

Lightning called for her to come back, but she picked up the pace and left him alone.

Later that night, as the rain poured down, Mack slept beneath an overpass and snored loudly. Inside the trailer, Lightning watched television, flipping mindlessly through the channels until he landed on a familiar show.

"Champion for the Ages Chick Hicks here, coming to you live from Chick Hicks Studios, where I'm joined once again by next-gen racing expert Natalie Certain."

"Thanks, Chick. Piston Cup Champion Jackson Storm set a new record today when he pulled off the fastest lap ever recorded: an unprecedented 213 miles an hour...."

Lightning watched as footage showed Storm sailing around the track. Then Chick and Natalie appeared on the screen.

"Wow!" said Chick Hicks. "So, whaddaya think, Certain? Stormy boy gonna start the season with another win?"

"Highly likely, Chick," said Natalie. "Based on his recent run times, and expected track temperatures on race day, Storm's chances of winning are" – a ding sounded on the screen behind them – "95.2 per cent."

Chick Hicks chuckled. "That low, huh?" he said. Then he looked at the audience. "Oh, and in case you missed it –" Humiliating footage of Lightning at the Crazy Eight track flashed behind Chick. "The talk of the track tonight is Lightning McQueen finding yet another way to embarrass himself – at a demolition derby! Whoa! Almost makes me feel sorry for the guy – not really! Here's what his new sponsor had to say."

Sterling appeared on the screen.

"Everyone relax! The 95's gonna race. Lightning's just taking a somewhat ... unconventional approach to this race is all. It's one of the things his fans love about him."

"Yeah, right!" said Chick Hicks, back on the screen. "Talk about humiliating! If I were old Ka-chow, I wouldn't even bother showing up in Florida."

"That could be for the best, Chick. Even if he does race, Lightning's probability of winning is" – another ding sounded as Natalie announced what was illuminated behind her on the screen – "one-point-two per cent."

"Wow!" said Chick.

"Numbers never lie," said Natalie. "I'm willing to predict tonight that Lightning McQueen's racing career will be over within the week. It might even be over now."

Lightning clicked off the television with a heavy sigh.

CHAPTER 14

Back in Radiator Springs, Mater turned off the lights in the tow shop, closing it down for the night. He'd been tinkering with recycled objects, one of his favourite activities. Just then, an unexpected light flickered by the main building. He started singing to himself as he drove over to check it out. The light belonged to his video phone. He moved closer and beamed at the sight of the caller ID: "My best friend, Ka-chow."

Inside Mack's trailer, Lightning looked at the screen, waiting for Mater's face to appear. Finally, it did – albeit a little crooked.

Mater grinned. "Well, hey there, buddy!"

Lightning laughed. "Mater!" He was so happy to see his friend and instantly felt a little better.

"Y'know, I was just thinkin' of you, and here ya are, lookin' right at me!" Mater said, his face only half visible to Lightning. "You see me okay? Hang on a second, there.... Hold on, let me see here." Mater moved the device around, trying to get his whole face on camera. "That better?"

"Lookin' you straight in the eye, pal," said Lightning,

smiling as he looked at Mater's eye, which now filled the entire screen. "Hey, sorry about calling so late."

"Shoot, not for me, it's not!" said Mater. "I'm always burnin' that midnight oil." He messed with the screen again and finally got it right. "So get me caught up on everything!"

"Well, actually, I was kinda hopin' I might hear what's goin' on back home," said Lightning.

"Well, not much ... not if you don't count Sarge and Fillmore tryin' to run the tyre shop. But tell Luigi not to worry – Sarge is gonna track down every last tyre that Fillmore done gived away."

Lightning smiled.

"Other than that, everything's good," added Mater.

"How's Sally?" asked Lightning.

"Oh, she's fine. Keepin' busy at the Cone. She misses ya. Well, shoot! We all do when you're on the road."

"Yeah. You know, I've been thinkin' about that. You know ... what we should do when I'm not on the road any more."

"What do you mean 'not on the road'?" asked Mater.

"Well, you know. Mater, I can't do this for ever."

"Huh?" said Mater.

Lightning sighed. "I'm just not getting anywhere with the training. If anything, I've gotten slower, not faster."

"Ahhh, shoot, buddy, it'll work out," said Mater. "Just tell me what the problem is. I'll stay right here with ya till we fix it."

"That's just it, Mater. I don't know! And I feel like

I'm all out of ideas."

"Hmmm, all right, lemme think. OH! You know what I'd do?"

"What?" asked Lightning.

"I don't know. I got nuthin'." Mater paused. "I guess I ain't Doc when it comes to that."

"I would give anything to talk to him right now," said Lightning.

"Yep, there was nobody smarter than old Doc. Well, except for maybe whoever taught him," Mater mused.

"Yeah. Wait. What?"

"I mean, everybody was taught by somebody, right?"

Lightning sat on those words as Mater rattled on.

"Take my cousin Doyle. He taught me how to sing and whistle at the same time. He was very musical that way."

"Smokey," Lightning said to himself. "Mater, you're brilliant!"

"Ah, well, it's all about the shape of yer teeth."

"I gotta go to Thomasville!" shouted Lightning.

"Oh. Well, good. You know me, buddy. I'm always happy to help. Think I'm better at that than most folks. You know, talkin' and stuff."

Lightning had a smile in his voice when he said goodbye to his best friend.

CHAPTER 15

The next morning, Cruz snaked along a winding country road as Mack pulled up beside her. She glanced at him for a moment, then fixed her gaze back on the road. Mack pulled forward, opened the trailer gate, and kept pace right in front of Cruz. In the trailer, Lightning faced Cruz.

"You won't talk me out of this, Mr McQueen," said Cruz, continuing to drive. "I'm going back to the training centre. I resign as your trainer."

"All right," said Lightning, upbeat. "I accept your resignation.... Bye."

Lightning closed the gate and Cruz looked up at him, a little surprised. Then he opened the gate again. "But since you've cleared your calendar, why don't you come with us?"

"Why?"

"I'm looking for someone named Smokey. Hopin' he can help me – and maybe you, too."

Cruz pondered this for a brief moment, but eventually refused.

Lightning moved deeper into Mack's trailer and slid out the trophy from the demolition derby, now glued back together. "I fixed it," he said, peeking out to see her reaction. "Come on."

"You know what? No. Thanks anyway, but I'm done."

"Okay – but maybe this will change your mind!" said Lightning.

Luigi hit a button on a boom box, and music with a dance beat kicked on. Lightning lowered the tailgate ramp. "First, I'm gonna loosen up these ancient joints!" he said as he rolled towards her, moving to the beat.

"No!" said Cruz. "Please don't."

Lightning continued the dance exercises on the ramp, speaking to the beat of the music, just like she had at the training centre. "I'm sorry, I'm sorry, I'm sorry I yelled! It wasn't your fault that I almost got killed."

"Stop!" shouted Cruz.

"But now you're leaving and won't get on the ramp. You won't get on the ramp," he continued. He leaned in and whispered, "Don't make me do this the whole freakin' way."

Cruz smiled, softening. "All right. I'll go – just stop!"

Lightning backed up, making room for her to drive into Mack's trailer. She smiled as she rolled in, the gate closing behind her.

Hours later, they were still inside Mack's trailer, heading down the highway. "How do you know Smokey's gonna be here?" asked Cruz.

"I don't," Lightning replied.

"Oh." Cruz was silent for a moment. "Do you know if he's even alive?"

"Nope."

"Okay … so, tell me this," Cruz began. "How do you know if it's Smokey? Is there some –"

Mack turned down a small country road and suddenly they were in front of a dense forest.

"Wait!" shouted Lightning, spotting a large wooden sign. "Mack! Pull over! Back it up!"

Mack obeyed, and Lightning rolled out with Cruz behind him. He inspected the old rickety sign. In faded paint was Welcome to Thomasville, Home of the Fabulous Hudson Hornet.

"Good to see you, Doc," Lightning said to himself, taking a moment. "Hey, Cruz," he began. "You wanna check out the track of the greatest racer of all time?"

"Aren't we supposed to be looking for Smokey?" Cruz asked.

Lightning moved behind the sign. In the distance he could see the classic Thomasville Speedway. Cruz followed him, and the two stood quietly, taking in the sight.

"Sure you have time for this?" asked Cruz.

"For this," said Lightning, "I do."

Lightning pushed against an old door, but it was locked. He pushed harder, and the chain holding the door gave way. With Cruz behind him, they entered a quiet tunnel and drove through. When they emerged on the other side, they slowly entered the speedway. Lightning stopped at the edge of the track, taking a deep breath and paying his respects to the sacred place. As he looked around, he didn't see the puddles, weeds or broken grandstands that were actually there. Instead he saw the track as it was in its glory days, back when Doc was a young racing car.

Lightning placed his tyres on the track and moved them back and forth in the dirt. "Wow, if this track could talk," said Lightning quietly. Then he slowly turned and found the starting line. "Cruz, whaddaya say? Let's take a lap." Vroooom! His engine thundered, and he took off. Unable to resist the offer, Cruz raced after him, laughing.

As Lightning led Cruz around the track, they whipped around and spurred each other on. They laughed, clearly having a blast. Cruz attempted the "turn right to go left" drifting move that she'd failed to execute at the demolition derby. Only this time, she did it beautifully! Cruz laughed out loud. She was thrilled!

"Ooooh! You nailed it!" Lightning said.

"Way easier without the school bus of death trying to kill us!"

"No kidding!"

As they came around the next turn, Lightning saw the ghostly silhouette of a car parked in the middle of the track. He broke hard, his tyres screeching. He stopped just short of slamming into an old Hudson pickup truck.

"Starting to think I might never meet you," said the truck, looking Lightning up and down.

Lightning's eyes popped. "Smokey?" he asked.

"He's alive," said Cruz.

Smokey fixed his gaze on Lightning. "I know why you're here," he said. Then he rolled over and Lightning scooted in, ready to hear his words of wisdom. "You're thirsty."

Lightning looked confused as Smokey drove off, leaving them standing there. They exchanged a look and hurried after Smokey, wondering where they were going.

CHAPTER 16

Smokey led them into town and up to the door of a bar called the Cotter Pin. There was an ancient sign on the top of the building with the bar's name. "I tell you what, these folks are gonna get a kick outta meeting Hud's boy," said Smokey.

He threw open the door, and warm, happy, old-fashioned music was playing inside. Vintage cars were everywhere, sitting together, chatting and clinking oil cans. Lightning and Cruz felt as if they had stepped back in time!

"Hey." called Smokey, causing the place to fall silent. "Act civilized. We got company." Everyone inside turned to see who it was, and then chirped with excitement.

Smokey exchanged pleasantries with a few regulars, then led a smiling Lightning and Cruz towards a corner booth in the back. Smokey began chatting with the cars at the table, but Lightning and Cruz stayed back. Lightning's jaw dropped when he saw who was there. "Would ya look at that," he mused.

"What? Who?" asked Cruz.

"Three of the biggest racing legends ever. Junior 'Midnight' Moon. River Scott. Louise 'Barnstormer' Nash. They all raced with Doc," whispered Lightning.

"Louise 'Barnstormer' Nash," Cruz repeated. "She had thirty-eight wins. She's amazing."

Lightning and Cruz headed over to the table to join Smokey and his friends.

"Well, as I live and breathe. If it ain't Lightning McQueen," said Louise.

"Ms Nash, it's a pleasure to meet –" started Lightning.

"You've had a tough year, haven't ya?" Louise interrupted.

Lightning was a bit taken aback and began to stammer, "Oh – oh … uh … Well, heh, yeah –"

"Shouldn't you be runnin' practice laps in Florida by now?" asked River Scott.

Lightning continued to fumble over his words. "Well, yeah … sure … but, uh –"

"He's here to steal our secrets," said Junior Moon.

"Lookin' for your lost mojo, huh?" said River.

Lightning couldn't believe their brutal honesty. "Wow. You don't mince words around here, do you?" he said, turning to Smokey.

Smokey chuckled. "The truth is always quicker, kid."

As the evening wore on, the gang stayed in the corner booth, talking and having a good time. A forklift named Sweet Tea sang a smooth tune, and Guido and Luigi watched in amazement.

"Guido! She's an angel!" said Luigi, unable

to take his eyes off her.

Meanwhile, Lightning and Cruz were fascinated by the stories the Legends told. They soaked up every word.

"Lou won't admit this, but she used to have serious eyes for Hud!" said River.

"Ohhhh, really?" asked Lightning.

"Even if I did, it wouldn't have mattered. Hud didn't like fast women … and that left me out!" said Louise.

Everyone laughed.

"But ol' Lou wasn't just fast. She was fearless," said River.

"The second I saw my first race, I knew I just had to get in there. 'Course, the fellas in charge didn't like the idea of a lady racer showin' 'em up, so they wouldn't let me have a number."

"What did you do?" asked Cruz.

"I stole one!" said Louise. Lightning and Cruz couldn't believe it, and exchanged a look of shock. "Life's too short to take no for an answer. Right, River?" added Louise.

"If we had waited for an invitation, we mighta never raced," River replied.

"That's right," said Louise. "And once we got on the track, we didn't want to leave."

"I think that's how Doc felt too," said Lightning.

"Ain't that the truth," said Louise.

River smiled. "You shoulda seen him when he first came to town, shiny blue paint – not just the Hudson Hornet. He was already calling himself …"

"The Fabulous Hudson Hornet!" they all said

together, laughing at the memory.

"Hoo-hoo! Oh, did we ever ride him on that," said Louise.

"Not for long," said Junior Moon.

"Hud was the fastest racer this side of the Mississippi," said River.

"Until he wasn't," added Smokey. Lightning was surprised to hear Smokey say that. "Everything changed when the rookie showed up," he said.

"What happened?" asked Lightning.

While Smokey spoke, Lightning imagined the scene in his mind. A race was in full swing, and Doc was working his way up through a pack of cars. "Took Hud all of no time to work his way through the best racers in both Carolinas. Past River. Past Lou. Even Junior," Smokey said. He mentioned the friendly competitiveness they had with each other back then. It sounded a lot like the relationships Lightning had with Cal, Bobby, and Brick.

"But there was still the rookie to deal with," Smokey said.

He told how the rookie took the lead, with the finish line in view. Doc dug deep, pushing himself until he was right behind him. But then the rookie slammed Doc hard into the wall. "Once. Twice. Hud knew he couldn't outrun him. He'd have to out-think him," Smokey continued.

He then described one of the most incredible moves of Doc's racing career. Doc drove up the side of the wall, pushed off it, and then flipped over the rookie! Smokey said Doc's roof actually touched the rookie's roof as he rolled over him. Then Doc gracefully touched down on all four tyres and sailed for the chequered flag.

"That rookie never saw Hud coming," said Smokey when he was done.

Lightning couldn't believe it. "Doc did that?" he said.

"He flipped over another racer?" asked Cruz.

"Yeah, he put on quite a show that day," Smokey said.

The Legends laughed, enjoying the memory of those good times.

"Couldn't wipe the smile off his face for a week after that," Louise said.

Lightning sat thinking about Smokey's story and the Doc he remembered. He wanted to join in the fun, but instead a deep sadness came over him. "I wish I could've seen him like that," Lightning said.

"Like what?" Smokey asked.

"So happy."

With that, Lightning wheeled out of the bar.

CHAPTER 17

Smokey followed Lightning outside. "You didn't come all this way for a pint of oil, did you?" he asked.

"I need your help, Smokey," Lightning confessed.

"What kind of help?"

"That's just it; I'm not sure. All I know is if I lose in Florida, it's over for me." Lightning slumped. "What happened to Doc will happen to me."

"What did happen to him?"

"You know. Racing was the best part of his life. And when it ended, he ... well, we both know he wasn't the same after that."

"Is that what you think?" Smokey asked.

Lightning blinked. His silence was answer enough.

"C'mon," Smokey said. "I want to show you something."

Smokey drove and Lightning followed, not wanting to miss a moment. As they rode beneath the moonlight, Lightning hung on Smokey's every word. "You got the first part right," he started. "The crash broke Hud's body – and the 'no more racing' broke his heart. He cut himself off. Disappeared.... Son of a gun didn't talk to me for fifty years...." His voice trailed off and Lightning stayed close. Eventually, they came upon Smokey's garage. He opened the rolled-up door and ushered Lightning inside. "But then one day, the letters started comin' in, and every last one of 'em was about you."

As Lightning entered the space, he couldn't believe his eyes. An entire wall of the garage was devoted to him and Doc. There were treasures plastered everywhere – letters, pictures, newspaper clippings. The memories of Doc came flooding in so powerfully, it was as if he was physically there. Lightning was overwhelmed.

"Hud loved racin'.... But coachin' you? I'd never seen the old grump so happy," Smokey said.

Lightning's eyes travelled to a photo of himself – happily clutching his very first Piston Cup. And off to the side, gazing back at him with pride from under his crew chief headset, was Doc – smiling from ear to ear.

"Racing wasn't the best part of Hud's life," Smokey revealed. "You were."

Lightning couldn't believe what he was hearing. The weight of Smokey's words was a lot to take in. Smokey knew when a car needed to be alone, and he softly rolled out of the garage – giving Lightning space to think. As he pored over the photographs and mementos, flashbacks of Doc started playing out in front of him.

All of a sudden, they were in Doc's garage in Radiator Springs.

"So, you ready to blow a little carbon, there, boy?" Doc asked.

"Yes, I am!" Lightning replied.

An amused Doc looked down at Lightning, stuck in the gully.

"You give it too much throttle, you're in the tulips," Doc said.

Doc balanced several cans of oil on his bonnet.

"You may wanna take notes on this one," Doc said, laughing.

A race around Willy's Butte in Radiator Springs....

Finally, Lightning returned to the present moment and stared at a photo of Doc and himself on Smokey's wall. He could hear Doc's voice again, loud and clear: "You got a lotta stuff, kid."

When Lightning was ready, he exited the garage – and found Smokey waiting. "Hud saw somethin' in you that you don't even see in yourself," Smokey said. "Are you ready to go find it?"

Lightning gave him an enormous smile. "Yes, sir."

CHAPTER 18

Lightning rejoined Cruz and followed Smokey towards Thomasville Speedway. The stadium lights popped on, one by one, as the three of them entered.

"All right. Lesson one!" Smokey shouted. "You're old. Accept it."

"I told him that," chimed Cruz.

Smokey chuckled and whispered loudly to Cruz, "He's probably losing his hearing."

Cruz began to repeat what Smokey had said: "He said you're old —"

"I heard him," said Lightning.

"You'll never be as fast as Storm," said Smokey. "But you can be smarter than him."

"Okay, what do I —"

"They said you were in a demolition derby," Smokey said, looking over Lightning's frame.

"Yeah, it was terrible, and I almost —"

"Ya sure?" Smokey asked. "'Cause there's not a scratch on ya." He paused, letting that sink in. "Funny what a racer can do when he's not overthinking things," he added.

"So … hold on – you want me to be smarter … without thinking so much," said Lightning.

"Exactly!" said Smokey.

Meanwhile, at the Florida International Super Speedway, Jackson Storm was already running practice laps – and continuing to impress everyone. Shannon Spokes, a correspondent for Racing Sports Network, was reporting live from the track: "Jackson Storm clocked 214 per hour today!" Right on cue, Storm ripped around the corner at an incredible rate. The crowd "oohed" in response.

Back in Thomasville, Lightning's training was finally taking shape. Clank! A silencer fell to the ground, and Cruz was lowered off a lift. She'd been outfitted with a new spoiler and racing tyres, and Guido had duct-taped a sloppy Jackson Storm 2.0 onto her sides. Much to everyone's surprise, Cruz looked like a real racer.

"You wanna beat Jackson Storm, you need someone to stand in for him – like a sparring partner," said Smokey.

It was obvious that Cruz was uncomfortable. Thankfully, the Legends cheered her on and helped her settle into her new look.

"All right, lookin' good," Louise called out. "Just like a racing car! You look just like Storm himself."

"I'm not so sure," Cruz answered back. "Just a trainer."

"Go ahead and gun it," said Smokey.

Cruz obeyed, and her engine roared to life.

"With no silencer, you even sound like Storm!" Smokey said.

"Uh, you're going down, Lightning," Cruz began, nervous at first. But she eventually found her rhythm. "Get that arthritis-riddled boot onto that track so I can put you into the old folks' home against your will!"

Everyone stared at her. Even Cruz was shocked by what she was capable of.

"How was that?" she asked timidly.

"That'll do," said Lightning.

Moments later, Lightning and Cruz lined up at the Speedway. "Here we go," said Smokey. "Now, in Florida, you'll be starting in the back of the pack, since ya missed qualifying." He nodded at Cruz. "Storm here will be up at the pole. I'll give you three laps to catch her."

"Go through the entire field in three laps?" Lightning protested.

"You wanna beat Storm or not?" said Smokey.

"Yes, of course I do –"

"Well, then," Smokey said, "GO!"

Lightning and Cruz took off, racing around the track. Lightning tried his hardest, but couldn't even get close to Cruz. She crossed the finish line way ahead of him. Cruz couldn't help it – she squealed with delight when she realized she'd won.

"All right," said Smokey. "Looks like we got some work to do."

Lightning and Cruz quickly realized that Smokey's training was the opposite of what racers were getting at Sterling's state-of-the-art racing centre. Lightning found himself out on a quiet country road, hitched to a giant trailer. Cruz was right beside him, hitched to a trailer of her own.

"Okay, go ahead!" yelled Smokey.

Lightning tried with all his might to pull the heavy load. "It won't budge," Lightning said with a lot of effort.

"This has nothing to do with horsepower," Smokey barked. "It's about managing torque and not spinning your wheels!"

Right on cue, both Lightning and Cruz spun their tyres pitifully, unable to move the trailers an inch.

Later, Smokey had Lightning and Cruz try a different exercise. He had Guido on the back of a truck, throwing giant hay bales at their heads. Lightning and Cruz dodged and dived as best they could. Everyone was shouting over the sound of the engines.

"The reflexes are the first thing to go!" yelled Smokey.

Just then, a hay bale smacked Lightning square in the face.

A little while later, Lightning and Cruz found themselves in a pasture where some tractors were peacefully motoring around. Smokey rolled over to a nearby gate and closed it.

"Sneak through that window!" he said.

"What does that mean?" asked Cruz.

Before she could get an answer, Smokey yelled, "Go!" He revved his engine suddenly, scaring the tractors! They went wild, running in every direction. Lightning and Cruz shrieked, stuck in the middle of the chaotic stampede!

"Not cool, man, not cool!" shouted Cruz.

During another training session, Smokey took Lightning and Cruz back out on the country road. Again, Smokey had Lightning pull the trailer, but this time he had to pull it with Smokey, Cruz, Luigi, Guido and the whole gang riding on top!

"You ain't gonna pass Storm, movin' like that!" yelled Smokey. "Dig for it! How about a little giddyup? Now come on! Hit it!"

Lightning panted as he tried to pick up the pace while pulling the heavy trailer.

Soon Smokey had Lightning line up on the track again, a quarter lap behind Cruz. Lightning raced hard and managed to close the gap a little more than before. But Cruz still won.

"Run it back," Smokey said.

Smokey had them race several times. With each effort, Lightning seemed to get closer, but Cruz always managed to beat him to the chequered flag.

"Do you even want to be out here?" Smokey shouted. "Only two days left, kid!" He told Lightning that if he wanted to win, he was going to have to work a lot harder.

Lightning was very, very frustrated. He thought he had

been working harder than ever, but it still didn't seem to be enough....

And he was now running out of time....

CHAPTER 19

Back at the Florida International Super Speedway, Storm was training on the simulator. He was moving extremely fast, and passed a red blur. "What was that?" he asked.

Storm's crew chief chuckled. "I put Lightning in there! Give ya some competition!"

"Put my grandma in next," Storm retorted. "She'll be faster!"

Meanwhile, in Thomasville, Lightning was as far away from high-tech machinery as he could get. That night, Smokey, Lightning and Cruz met up with the Legends at the drive-in theatre to watch racing footage of Doc. Up on the screen, Doc was in the middle of the pack, figuring out his next move. He was riding so close to the car in front of him, he was nearly touching it. Lightning and Cruz were completely enthralled, waiting to see what he would do next.

"See that?" asked Smokey. "Hud was a master of

letting the other cars do some of the work for him."

Junior Moon chimed in. "Doc used to say ya cling to 'em like you was two June bugs on a summer night."

They watched as Doc suddenly pulled out from behind the car and passed a young Junior. He flashed a smile when he skated by.

"Draughting?" said Lightning. "I've never had to do that."

"Yeah," said Smokey. "That's when you were fast. Now you're slow."

"And old," said River Scott.

"And rickety," said Louise.

"And dilapidated," said Junior Moon.

"Okay, okay! I get it!" Lightning exclaimed, ready to change the subject.

"The new you has to look for opportunities you never knew were there," Smokey added. Lightning watched the rest of the race, letting Smokey's words sink in.

The next day, Smokey had Lightning and Cruz back out in the pasture.

"Sneak through the window!" shouted Smokey, watching them struggle in the chaos of the herd.

Lightning spotted a small space between two tractors. He repeated Smokey's words to himself, and then it clicked. He had an idea.

"What?" asked Cruz, still completely confused.

"When a window opens, take it!" Lightning said. He started smoothly moving between the tractors. "*Whoa-ho!*" he shouted.

Lightning slalomed through the tractors with ease. Cruz tried to follow. She squealed as she watched, but after a couple of failed attempts, she swiftly raced between the two of them.

"I made it!" she shouted.

"All right!" said Lightning.

Later on, out on the country road, Lightning dodged bales of hay again with Cruz. All the Legends watched as this time, Lightning successfully avoided each obstacle.

Smokey then had Lightning line up on the track. "I said gun it!" he shouted. Guido waved the green flag, and Lightning revved his engine. He sped away – quicker than before – which forced a smile to creep across Smokey's grille. "All right. That didn't stink."

A little while later, Smokey had Lightning pull the trailer again – with everyone riding on top of it. Only this time, Lightning had to drag it uphill!

"Come on! Get on it!" yelled Smokey. "Catch Storm!"

Lightning panted, straining as he pulled them up the steep incline.

"Reach for your lunch!" said Cruz, cheering him on.

Determined, Lightning dug deep and used everything in him to reach the very top. Finally, he made it! Everyone on the trailer erupted into cheers, then slid down the other side of the hill – hooting, hollering and enjoying the ride.

Day turned to night, and Lightning and Cruz followed Smokey and the Legends into the woods. "This is where we cut our racing teeth," said Smokey.

Lightning and Cruz were intrigued as they wondered what Smokey had in mind for them next.

"In the woods?" Lightning asked.

"Let's just say the moon was always shining on us," River Scott said with a sly smile.

Lightning and Cruz didn't get it.

"If the moon didn't shine, we didn't have to go in – Oh, never mind!" Louise exclaimed.

"We ran moonshine, dummy!" Junior Moon screamed.

"Oooooh," said Lightning, finally understanding. But when the Legends suddenly turned off their headlights, he and Cruz were confused again!

"By the way, no lights," said Smokey. "Instinct only."

With that, the Legends raced off into the woods, yelling and cheering. Lightning and Cruz followed, but they moved much slower, dodging trees and boulders in the dark. Without lights, it was difficult to see – and it was terrifying!

Eventually, Lightning began to manoeuvre with more ease, and it became more fun than scary. "*Wooooo!*" he shouted. A few branches scraped against his side, gashes appearing in the high-tech wrap that Sterling had given Lightning at the racing centre. As he drove, the entire wrap gave way and ripped off, revealing the paint job that Ramone had given Lightning the day he left Radiator Springs. And in no time, Cruz and Lightning found themselves racing past the Legends!

"Hey!" said Louise.

"*Whooo-hoo-hooo-hooo!*" shouted Lightning.

For the first time in weeks – under the moon and surrounded by laughter – Lightning raced for the fun of it. In that moment, he felt that anything was possible.

CHAPTER 20

Outside the Florida International Super Speedway, reporters were interviewing next-gen racers, asking for their opinions of Lightning McQueen. "Lightning's still not here?" said one. "Didn't he pull this when he was a rookie? At least that's what my grandfather told me."

"Maybe it's best he doesn't show up, you know, after how last season ended," said another racer.

"Lemme put it this way," another Next Gen chimed in. "I'm not losing any sleep wondering where Lightning McQueen is."

Back at the Thomasville Speedway, Smokey called out to Lightning and Cruz: "All right! We've got time for one last race!"

Mack urged them to hurry things along. They needed to get to Florida.

"Maybe I should take it easy on you this time!" said Cruz, taunting him as they took their marks.

"Don't even think about it," said Lightning.

All of a sudden, Smokey yelled, "Go!" and they took

off! Lightning could feel himself moving faster. He was stronger than before, gaining ground and closing the gap between him and Cruz.

After the first turn, Lightning managed to get right behind her. The Legends watched with excitement. It was going to be a close race!

"C'mon, boy!" Smokey muttered under his breath.

Managing his torque, Lightning catapulted himself around Cruz and took the lead! But she quickly took it back, boxing him out. He dodged and went the other way – suddenly ahead again! They were neck and neck as they reached the straightaway.

Finally, Lightning saw his chance. He gunned his engine, gave it everything he had, and passed Cruz! It was his final push of the race, and it looked as though he would win.

But Cruz dug deep, and in a flash of speed, passed him and pulled away. Lightning couldn't believe it! He had fallen behind, and there was no way to catch her. In his mind, he could hear Darrell Cartrip saying, "Lightning is fading! Lightning is fading! Fading fast!" He remembered the terrible accident that had changed his life.

Cruz left him in the dust and crossed the finish line. Feeling a jolt of excitement, she celebrated. "*Whooooo-hoooo*! Yes! That was awesome!" She stopped herself when she realized what had happened – and what it meant for Lightning.

Lightning slowed to a stop, shocked and disappointed. Smokey and the Legends looked down as everyone felt the weight of Lightning's failure. He looked at Cruz for a moment and then rolled away.

"Sorry, I didn't mean to ..." Cruz said, feeling horrible.

Lightning rolled over to Smokey and the Legends. He took a deep breath, not sure what to say or do.

"Uh, boss?" Mack asked. He once again reminded Lightning that they needed to get on the road.

"I want to thank everyone for the training," Lightning finally said. And after a short pause, "We, um, better get going to Florida."

CHAPTER 21

High energy pulsed through the Florida International Super Speedway as fans filled the stands and teams prepared for the big race. Bob Cutlass, Darrell Cartrip and the rest of the announcers chattered with excitement.

"Welcome, fans, to racing's greatest day!" said Bob Cutlass. "We're beachside for the Florida 500. A quarter million spectators are here to kick off a new season of exciting Piston Cup racing."

"That's right!" echoed Darrell Cartrip. "Forty-three cars are awaiting today's intense contest of strategy, skill, and most of all, speed. This crowd is in for one great day of racing!"

Back in Radiator Springs, Lizzie, Red and Sheriff were watching television, waiting for the race to begin. "They're gonna race on a beach?" shouted Lizzie.

Inside the booth, Natalie Certain joined Bob Cutlass and Darrell Cartrip. She gestured to her board, which was covered with dozens of stats. "I've never seen the numbers line up for Storm like they do today, Bob," she said. "Storm should be 98.6 per cent unstoppable."

In Thunder Hollow, Miss Fritter and her Crazy Eight racer friends were at their local bar watching the race coverage on TV. They cheered at the sound of Lightning's name. "WHIPPLEFILTER!" shouted Miss Fritter. "*WHOO-HOO!*"

Moments before the race, teams anxiously hustled to prepare, checking and rechecking everything to make sure they were ready, while the announcers discussed the big questions that were on everyone's mind.

"We've heard stories of the unusual way Lightning McQueen trained to get here," said Darrell Cartrip. "Now the question is – did it work?"

Lightning sat inside his quiet trailer, trying to focus. "Speed. I. Am. Speed?" he said nervously. He let out a shaky sigh. "No, I'm not."

A loud knock on the trailer door shook his attention. "Hey, boss." It was Mack. "They just called for the racers to report to the grid!"

Lightning took another deep breath and headed out. As he passed his pit, he wheeled by Jeff Gorvette.

"Hey, McQueen," Jeff called out. "Good luck out there. Win one for us old guys," he said.

Lightning laughed, but it wasn't quite genuine. "Will do, Jeff," he replied.

The gang from Radiator Springs was in the pit, decked out in their 95 garb. And Mater wore a giant Piston Cup hat, complete with the number 95 written on it.

"Whoo-hoo! Hey there, Buddy!" Mater said.

"Hey, guys," said Lightning.

"You sure you're up for this?" asked Sally. This was not the confident Lightning that she expected to see, and it worried her.

"Yeah, yeah, absolutely," said Lightning.

Cruz rolled up, breaking the tension. She and Lightning shared a quick smile.

"Thanks for sticking around," Lightning said.

"Yeah, well, I wouldn't miss it for anything," said Cruz.

Just then, Storm passed by. He stopped to take a long look at Cruz, scoffing at the 'Storm 2.0' duct tape that was still on her side. "Look at that," he said. "That is a nice costume. It's so great to meet my number-one fan."

"She's not a fan, Storm," said Lightning.

Storm turned to Lightning with a phony smile. "Oh! Hey, champ!" he said in a fake-friendly tone. "I hear you're sellin' mud flaps after today." Without giving Lightning a chance to respond, he turned away and started off. Then he called back, "Hey! Put me down for the first case!"

Lightning tried his best not to let Storm's cruel words bother him as he headed towards the track. He lined up in the last position and began nervously scrubbing his tyres. Maddy, the same adoring young fan from before, spotted him and yelled out his name. "LIIIIIGHTNIIIIING! LIIIIIGHTNIIIIING MCQUEEEEEEN!"

Lightning flashed her a timid smile and scanned the crowd. He had never felt so uncertain. The last thing he wanted was to let his fans down. He closed his eyes, took another deep breath, and tried to reset himself.

But then a jolt of irritation rippled through his body as he heard Sterling's voice come through the headset. "Hey, Lightning!"

He looked over towards the pit, surprised to see Sterling there, wearing a headset of his own. "Oh. Hey, Mr Sterling," Lightning replied.

"To the future, eh, champ?"

"Yeah," Lightning said nervously. "To the future."

Then he heard Smokey's voice through the headset. "Hey, just focus on what you're here to do, kid," he said.

The sight of Smokey on the crew-chief stand comforted Lightning. "Thanks, Smokey," he said. He set his sights ahead, ready for the start of the race. The green flag dropped and Lightning took off!

"Boogity, boogity, boogity, let's go racin'!" said Darrell Cartrip.

The crowd cheered as Lightning propelled forward, getting a good start, all things considered. "There ya go, kid!" said Smokey. "Now show 'em how the old guys race."

Lightning grinned and his nerves calmed a bit. He concentrated and started passing racers. In the pit, Sally and Mater exchanged a smile – relieved, happy, and proud that Lightning was doing so well.

"Lightning McQueen is making steady progress in the early part of this race," said Bob Cutlass.

Natalie Certain chimed in. "Well, it won't be enough to catch Storm."

"Maybe not, but considering he started dead last, he's not doing half bad out there!" added Darrell Cartrip.

Lightning continued to race his best, pushing ahead of more and more cars. In fact, he moved up from last place to the mid-twenties.

"Not too shabby!" said Smokey. "You keep this up, and you'll finish in the top ten!"

"Top ten's not gonna cut it, Smokey," said Lightning, determined to win. "I gotta go all the way!"

"Okay, then. So dig in! Remember your training. Then find Storm and chase him down!"

Cruz yelled up to Smokey. "Oh! Tell him he has three laps to catch me!"

"Cruz says you've got three laps to –" said Smokey.

"Yeah!" said Lightning. "I heard her!"

Just then, Sterling rolled over to Cruz and sternly told her to head back to the racing centre.

"But why?" she asked.

"Cruz, you've got no reason to be here. Just go do your job and get Kurt up to speed for the race next weekend. Um, wait, not Kurt. He's the bug guy, right? The other one – Ronald. Yes!"

Lightning heard every word as their conversation continued. "I want to stay and watch –"

Sterling interrupted her. "Not gonna happen, Cruz. Now go."

"But Mr McQueen still has a chance!" said Cruz.

"JUST DO YOUR JOB!" Sterling shouted.

Cruz was startled by his explosive reaction.

"And take off that spoiler and those racing tyres. You look ridiculous!" he said. Cruz started to leave, and Sterling yelled after her, "You're a trainer, remember? Not a racer!"

Cruz sadly turned to go. "Yes, sir," she said.

Thoughts of Cruz suddenly flooded Lightning's mind as he heard Sterling's cruel words. He remembered some of the unkind things he'd said to Cruz after Thunder Hollow. "If you were a racer, you'd know what I'm talking about! But you're not! So you don't!" He thought about how she had turned into Storm 2.0, and he remembered watching her for the first time, racing on the simulator. He realized how quickly she'd learned to race on the beach and drift around the Thomasville Speedway. He remembered how shocked he was by her words: "I've wanted to become a racer for ever. Because of you!" He thought about how she'd beaten him in every one of their practice races – even when he had pulled ahead. Lastly, he recalled Cruz telling him about her first race and her decision to leave before the race even started. "When they started their engines, that's when I realized I'd never be a racer. It was my one shot, and I didn't take it."

Suddenly, he snapped back to the present moment and panicked. His eyes desperately scanned the crowd, looking for Cruz. But just as he spotted her leaving the stadium, there was a crash on the track!

"Wreck in turn three! Go low, go low!" Smokey advised.

Lightning deftly navigated around the wrecked and

stalled cars. He then called out for Smokey, "I need Cruz!"

"Never mind that now, kid –"

"No!" shouted Lightning. "I need her back here. Now! Get her back!" he said as he rolled into the pits.

Out in the car park, Cruz was slowly making her way back to the training centre. She was listening to the race on the radio, growing more and more concerned about Lightning. Then Hamilton's voice broke her concentration. "Hamilton, here. Call from Chester Whipplefilter."

"Chester Whi – Mr McQueen?" asked Cruz.

Moments later, Lightning was barking out orders to his crew in the pits. "Get ready, guys. Luigi! Guido – tyres! Fillmore – fuel!"

As Cruz entered, she took in the chaotic scene and was still terribly confused. "Okay, I'm here. What's going on?"

Luigi, Guido and Fillmore started towards Lightning, but he called them off. "No, no, no. Not me, her," he said, gesturing to Cruz.

"What's she doing back here?" yelled Sterling.

"Come on, guys! Get her set up. Quickly!" shouted Lightning.

The crew rushed towards Cruz and immediately got to work.

"Wait, what's happening?" asked Cruz, still bewildered.

Lightning spotted Ramone and called him over. "You got your paints?" he asked.

"You know I do," answered Ramone.

As all the other racers finished their pit stops and pulled

out onto the track, Lightning's crew picked up the pace, working as quickly as possible on Cruz.

"I don't understand it!" said Darrell Cartrip, looking on from the booth. "Lightning McQueen's just sittin' there. Something must be wrong."

"Mr McQueen?" asked Cruz, begging for an explanation.

"Today's the day, Cruz," said Lightning. "You're getting your shot."

"What?" asked Cruz.

"I started this race, and you're gonna finish it," he said.

As Lightning's plan finally registered, a smile overtook Smokey's face.

Sterling frowned. "No!" he shouted. "She'll damage the brand! She's just a trainer!"

"No – she's a racer," said Lightning, looking proudly at Cruz. "Just took me a while to see it."

"You can't do that!" said Sterling. "That can't be legal!"

Smokey chuckled. "The rules only say the number has to be out there. Doesn't say who has to wear it."

"No!" Sterling fumed as he started towards Cruz, but Mater got in his way.

"Did I ever tell you I love your mud flaps?" said Mater, blocking Sterling.

"Outta my way, bumpkin!" snapped Sterling, trying to get around him. But Mater shuffled along, matching his every move, keeping him from getting to Cruz.

"Got my fishin' flaps, even got me some weddin' flaps, you know, just in case," chattered Mater.

Lightning saw that the rest of the racers were halfway around the track and he urged the crew to hurry. "We gotta get her out there! Come on – let's go!" he said.

"Tyres, check!" said Luigi.

"Gas, check!" said Fillmore.

"Ramone?" said Lightning.

Ramone looked up and dramatically dropped an empty paint can. It rolled across the concrete, making a hollow, tinny sound. Ramone backed away, revealing his latest masterpiece. "Eh, best I could do in the time frame, boss."

For a moment, they all gazed at Cruz, taking in her fantastic new look. "Yeah," said Lightning, impressed. "That'll work."

Cruz checked out the 95 on her side and felt a rush of emotions. "Why are you doing this?" she asked. "You said it yourself – this might be your last chance."

"Exactly!" Lightning exclaimed. "And if it is, that makes it my last chance to give you your first chance. And this time, I want you to take it."

Cruz was speechless. She smiled at Lightning and the light in her eyes thanked him more than words ever could.

The pack of cars followed the pace car around. "She's gotta beat that pace car out," said Smokey.

"NO! NO! NO!" shouted Sterling. "You can't do that." He tried to stop Cruz from going, but Mater was right there, blocking him again.

"Now or never," said Smokey.

Lightning looked Cruz straight in the eyes. "So what's it gonna be?" he said.

She took off, nervously burning out as she made her way towards the track.

"Whoa. Hey!" called Lightning. "Thirty-five miles per hour pit speed!"

"I knew that!" shouted Cruz. Then she joined the back of the pack under the yellow flag, ready to race.

CHAPTER 22

"I've never seen this before," announced Bob Cutlass. "Lightning McQueen's team has entered a different car sporting the 95!"

"I do not believe what I'm seeing!" said Darrell Cartrip.

In the pits, Storm's crew chief shot him a look. "You're watching this, right?"

"What, the girl in the costume?" said Storm. "You're kidding me! He put her in the race?"

"The green flag is out, and we are back to racing," said Bob Cutlass.

At the sight of the flag, the racers revved their engines and took off. The thunderous sound took Cruz by surprise, and she shuddered and slowed down. They revved again and she froze in her tracks, completely intimidated.

"Uh, Cruz, whaddaya doing?" asked Smokey. "Gotta go faster!"

Cruz didn't respond. She was too scared to move.

"Okay, call her Frances Beltline and tell her the school bus of death is after her!" said Lightning.

"What? No!" said Smokey.

"Trust me," said Lightning.

Smokey told her, and after a beat Cruz slowly smiled. "Oh, uh-huh. Right," she said.

"Okay, that was different," said Smokey. Then he noticed that Cruz was driving upright and not scrubbing her tyres. "Cruz, you're lookin' too tight," he said. "Loosen up!"

"Tell her she's a fluffy cloud," called Lightning.

"What? No," said Smokey.

"Smokey, tell her," insisted Lightning.

"Uh, Cruz, you are a fluffy cloud," Smokey said.

"Oh … yeah, too tight," said Cruz. "I'm a fluffy cloud. I'm a fluffy cloud," she chanted.

Cruz adjusted her form, and something inside her clicked. She sped up, joining the race, and blasted into the back of the pack! Excited by her speed and the rush of racing, she picked up her pace. As she made her first turn, she spun out a little and seemed astonished by her own speed.

"Anticipate your turns," said Smokey. "Cruz, get your head in the race."

Lightning thought about it and told Smokey, "Tell her she's on a beach and all the little crabbies have gone night-night."

"No!" grumbled Smokey. "I ain't saying that! You tell her!" Smokey gestured for Lightning to get onto the crew-chief podium. Without hesitation, he rushed up the ramp and put on the headphones. Down below, Mater bumped Sally and nodded up towards Lightning as he took the stand. The two exchanged a look. Lightning seemed like a natural on the podium. They smiled.

"All right, Cruz … the beach," said Lightning. "I need you to think of the beach!"

"Mr McQueen!" said Cruz. She was thrilled to hear him at the other end of the headset transmission.

"Yeah! Yeah! It's me. Remember the beach!"

"Oh, uh-huh. Pick a line. Stick to it. Got it!" Cruz said, gaining confidence.

She raced ahead and soon found herself smack in the middle of a pack of cars. They were all moving fast and as they raced against each other, trying to edge each other out, Cruz found herself getting bumped around. "This is nothing like the simulator!" she said.

"Told ya that," said Lightning.

"Not helping, crew chief!"

"You got every tool you need. Now remember Thomasville."

"Thomasville?"

"Yeah, sneak through the window."

"Now that I understand!" Smokey said with a chuckle.

Cruz looked around thoughtfully. She imagined that the cars in front of her were tractors. She spotted an opening between two and swiftly moved through! She continued to picture them that way as she skated between more and more of them, making her way through the pack.

"We're just learning that the racer replacing Lightning McQueen is Cruz Ramirez," said Bob Cutlass.

"Uh, she's a complete unknown," said Natalie Certain, sounding anxious. "I have no stats on her!"

Cruz continued to jockey through more gaps and soon reached a pack of Next Gens.

"This is her very first race!" shouted Darrell Cartrip.

"Okay, actually, it says here she does have one win under her belt," said Natalie Certain. "At a place called … Thunder Hollow?"

Back in Thunder Hollow, Miss Fritter and the Crazy Eight racers watching the television went berserk, cheering on their hometown track. "*Whooo-hooo!*"

Gaining strength and confidence, Cruz continued to work her way through the Next Gens. Lightning glanced over at Smokey, and the two exchanged a hopeful smile. With each car she passed, Cruz became increasingly daring.

"Okay, here we go," said Lightning, focusing back on Cruz and the track. "Watch your right."

"Got it. Thanks," said Cruz.

Lightning watched excitedly as he continued coaching her. He anticipated each potential challenge as if he were out there on the track himself. Cruz quickly reacted to his warnings and suggestions as the two worked together to tackle the race, completely in sync with each other.

"Now watch the tyre marbles along turn three," said Lightning. "They're slippery."

"Okay," said Cruz, adjusting herself.

"Bump comin' up on the inside – lift your body so you don't go airborne," said Lightning.

"Now?" asked Cruz.

"Yes, now!" said Lightning.

Cruz instantly adjusted and skated past the bump. The Next Gen behind her hit it and flew up into the air.

Cruz swiftly passed another car and grazed a wall. Lightning imitated the monotone sound of the simulator's voice. "You have hit a wall. You have hit a wall."

"Still not helping, crew chief!" she laughed.

When it was time to return to the pits, Cruz didn't slow down. Feeling great, she headed straight towards them. But, being inexperienced, she overshot.

"Uh, we're back here," Lightning said.

She rolled back and Guido speedily changed her tyres. When he finished, she zipped out onto the track!

"All right," said Lightning. "Pick 'em off one by one."

"All right!" said Cruz, completely focused on Lightning's words.

"He's behind ya!" said Lightning, bringing her attention to the Next Gen who was gaining on her. Cruz saw a window and went for it, cutting through another gap, creating more distance from the cars behind her.

"Smokey, you watching?" asked Lightning.

"Come on, girl!" said Smokey.

Cruz got past several more racers and steadily moved up on the leader board. The crowd buzzed with excitement over Cruz's performance. They cheered her on, rooting for her to win.

Over in Storm's pit, his crew chief checked in. "Just want to let you know, Cruz is moving up towards you," he said.

"Why should I care?" Storm asked.

"Well, because she's moved through the entire pack and now she's in the top ten!" the crew chief replied.

Lightning adjusted his headset. "Okay, okay — now you're coming up on the big boys." He was excited.

Cruz draughted behind a couple of cars and then finessed a creative move around the fourth-place car, catapulting herself all the way into third place. She was now only a short distance behind Storm.

"Cruz's in third," Storm's crew chief warned.

"Third? Huh. Okay," said Storm.

Everyone in the pits celebrated. "Cruz, this is unbelievable!" shouted Lightning. "You got three laps to go. Keep this pace, and you're in for a top-five finish!"

Cruz appeared on the large screen, and the crowd went wild, chanting her name. Storm slowed and shot a nasty look to Danny Swervez, who was in second place.

Lightning watched Storm closely. He slowed himself down, letting the second place car pass him. He was definitely up to something. Lightning narrowed his eyes as Storm dropped back even farther and rode beside Cruz.

"Hey! Costume Girl," Storm said. "You know, at first I thought you were just out here 'cause you were lost and your GPS was broken."

"Don't listen to him, Cruz!" shouted Lightning.

"You look great!" Storm said.

Cruz could hear Lightning's words of warning coming through the headset. "He's trying to get into your head!" he yelled.

"And out here, that's really all that matters," continued Storm. "It's important to look the part. You can't have everyone thinking that you don't deserve to be out here. No, they don't need to know what you and I already do. That you can play dress up all you want ... but you'll never be one of us."

With that, Storm pulled forward, leaving Cruz in the dust. She froze and started to slow. Storm effortlessly pulled past Danny and secured the lead.

"Cruz, did you see what happened there?" asked Lightning.

Cruz sighed. "Yeah. He got into my head."

"No. No! Listen to me. You got into his head! Don't you understand? He would never have done that if you didn't scare him."

"What?" Cruz asked.

"He sees something in you that you don't even see in yourself. You made me believe it, but now you gotta believe it, too."

"What's that?"

"That you're a racer."

Cruz was stunned by Lightning's words.

"Now, use that," Lightning added, using Cruz's favourite phrase.

A smile slowly crept across Cruz's face and her eyes focused with determination. She dug deep and gunned her engine.

CHAPTER 23

"And how far back is she now?" asked Storm smugly.

"Look behind you!" shouted Storm's crew chief.

Cruz was right on his tail. "Mornin', Storm!" she said.

"Wait, how did you –"

"Just your number-one fan back here draughting on your butt," Cruz said. "Nothing to be concerned about."

"Just like two June bugs on a summer night!" said Lightning, reciting one of Doc's famous sayings.

Storm tried to throw Cruz off by careening around. But she followed his every curve and turn. "This is fun!" said Cruz. "Hey, Hamilton –"

"Hamilton here," said the computerized voice.

"Call out our speed," she said.

"208 miles per hour, 207 miles per hour," said Hamilton.

"Would you stop that!" shouted Storm.

"205 miles per hour," said Hamilton.

"You're slowing down, Storm!" said Cruz, taunting him.

"Because you're takin' me off my line!" he yelled.

"Be careful, Cruz," said Lightning.

The white flag dropped for the last lap, a. continued to stick right on Storm.

"Last lap!" said Smokey.

"200 miles per hour. 199 miles per hour," announced Hamilton.

"Uh-oh," said Cruz. "My GPS is saying I have slow traffic in my way and that I should get in front of it!"

"You are not gonna win!" said Storm.

"Oh, you're angry," said Cruz.

"I am not angry," said Storm, clearly trying to control his temper.

"You know, you can use that anger to push through –"

"I SAID I AM NOT ANGRY!" screamed Storm.

As they approached the finish line, Cruz dropped back and over towards the inside of the track. Storm countered and edged in front of her. Without flinching, Cruz effortlessly flung herself through the gap along the wall and pulled ahead!

"Uh, I don't think so!" said Storm. He moved in close, smashing her into the wall! Sparks flew, and a loud scraping noise made the crowd wince as Cruz screamed in pain.

"Cruz!" shouted Lightning. "Get out of there!"

Lightning could barely watch as Storm pushed her harder and harder into the wall. "You don't belong on this track!" Storm yelled.

Cruz took a deep breath and answered with a loud, firm voice: "YES ... I ... DO!"

Suddenly, she drove up onto the wall, pushed off, and

flipped over Storm – just like Doc had done all those years ago! It was as if she were flying in slow motion. The whole crowd watched the thrilling moment in awe. Lightning's face lit up with a giant smile, and – BAM! – she touched down, crossing the finish line before Storm!

"It's Cruz Ramirez for the win!" shouted Bob Cutlass.

The crowd roared as Cruz let out a victory scream. "*Wa-hoooo-hoo-hoo!*"

"*Ooooh-ooo-hoo!*" shouted Lightning.

Maddy, the same young fan from the audience, revved her engine and exclaimed, "CRUZ RAMIREZ!"

The Radiator Springs gang cheered from the sidelines, and the Legends celebrated in the stands.

"Way to go, Cruz!" shouted Louise Nash.

Inside the Thunder Hollow Bar, Miss Fritter shouted gleefully, "Ohhhh, yeeeess!"

Back in Radiator Springs, Sheriff and Red were watching the race … and crying. Lizzie rolled over and said, "What'd I miss?"

Darrell Cartrip looked at Natalie Certain, still reeling from the shock of the outcome. "Man! Heckuva win!" he said as he gazed at the track below.

Natalie Certain looked up at her board with wonder. "Yeah," she said, looking down at the track with a grin. "Heckuva win."

Lightning watched proudly, trying to hold in his emotions as Cruz took a celebratory victory lap.

"Kid's got a lotta stuff, eh, Doc?" asked Lightning proudly. Then he turned his attention back to Cruz. "Go

ahead," he said into the headset. "Give 'em some smoke."

Cruz spun doughnuts in the infield, laughing and loving every second as the crowd cheered her on. She came back to Lightning, coughing from breathing in the smoke.

"You'll get used to that," he said.

Sterling, impressed by Cruz's win, changed his tune as he pushed through everyone to get to her. "Out of my way! C'mon, move it! Move!"

The Legends bristled at his rude behaviour, but he stayed the course.

"Cruuuuz," said Sterling, his voice dripping with admiration. "I knew you had something – and now look at you, a winner. I could use you as a racer on our team. We could make –"

"Sorry, Mr Sterling," said Cruz, cutting him off. "I would never race for you. I quit."

"Well, then race for me!" said a big, friendly voice. Tex Dinoco honked his horn as he approached. "Miss Cruz, I would be tickled pink to have ya race for team Dinoco," he said. "As you know, we have a long history of great racers ... 'cept for Cal."

"I'm still right here," said Cal.

"Hire her – I don't care," said Sterling. "Lightning, now that you're retired, I need you first thing Monday morning for a photo shoot."

"Yeah," said Lightning. "All right, Mr Sterling."

"Whoa," said Smokey. "Hang on."

They all looked up at the large screen to see "McQueen/Cruz" listed on the board as co-winners.

Sterling gasped....

"Why is my name up there?" asked Lightning.

"You started the race – that's how it works," said Smokey.

"Wait, wait, now wait a minute –" started Sterling.

"Uh, that was the deal," said Sally, rolling up. "Lightning wins, he decides when he's done racing." She flashed a smile. "I'm his lawyer."

"*Whoo-hoo*!" said Mater. "That was the deal. You are not a nice guy!" He leaned in and said, "Although, seriously, you do make a quality mud flap at an affordable price, but I would like you to leave, sir."

"You're all ridiculous," said Sterling. "I'm leaving." He turned and began to drive off, but suddenly stopped short. One of his tyres had been replaced with a fat one. Sterling screamed at the sight of it. "How did it –?"

Guido smirked as he blew smoke off his air spanner. "Pit stop."

Sally rolled over to Lightning. "So," she said, smiling at him. "You did it. You got the chance Doc never got. So … you gonna keep racing?"

Lightning gave Sally a knowing look. He loved everything about racing. But right now, there was only one place he wanted to be: home.

CHAPTER 24

The sun shone over Radiator Springs as Luigi gave an enthusiastic welcome to a small crowd. "Welcome, all, to historic Willy's Butte for today's great exhibition of speed!" he shouted.

The Radiator Springs gang, along with Tex, Smokey, Cruz's former next-gen trainees, and all the Legends cheered as Cruz rolled up, showing off her new look. She was sporting the Dinoco colours and logo – and had the number 51 painted on her sides.

"Thanks, guys!" said Cruz, beaming with pride.

"Go, go, Dinoco!" shouted Mater.

"Great number," said Smokey. "Was Lightning's idea. He felt Hud woulda wanted ya to have it."

"I love it," said Cruz.

"It's very old-school," added Sally.

"Did someone just say 'OLD-SCHOOL'?" Lightning approached with a new look of his own. The Fabulous Lightning McQueen was painted on his side, along with the number 95, and Crew Chief.

Sally gasped at the sight of him. He looked so different. She'd also never seen him so happy. "Tryin' something new. I like that, Mr Fabulous," she said.

"Suits you, boss," said Mack.

"Shiny new paint!" said River.

"Doc's back from college!" shouted Lizzie.

As Lightning joined Cruz at the starting line, she checked out his paint job. "Wow," said Cruz. "Subtle."

"Figured if I'm gonna be your crew chief, I better do it in style," said Lightning.

"And Mr Sterling's okay with this?" asked Cruz.

"He sold Rust-eze," Lightning replied. Then he turned to face his friends and shouted, "Thanks, Tex!"

The cars parted to make room for Tex Dinoco, who wheeled down the newly formed path. "Twarn't nothin'," he replied.

A small moment passed as Cruz took in the scene and realized what this meant for Lightning.

"Hope you got your drip pan," said Cruz.

"Got my drip pan, and I've taken my nap," he said.

"Bring it on, old man."

"Luigi?" Lightning asked.

Luigi smirked and shouted, "GO!"

Everyone hooted and hollered as Lightning and Cruz took off, racing around and having a blast, just like Lightning and Doc did so many years before. Lightning knew Doc would have been proud, and somehow, Doc felt close by ... which reassured Lightning that he was right where he was supposed to be.

The End